TWISTED IS THE CROWN

KEL CARPENTER

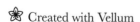

To those who don't let the past define them, and instead create their own future.

These violent delights have violent ends
And in their triumph die, like fire and powder,
Which as they kiss consume

William Shakespeare, *Romeo and Juliet, Act II,
Scene VI*

Cold Welcome

"If those you seek do not answer the door when you come calling, it is unwise to enter without invitation."
— *Quinn Darkova, vassal of House Fierté, fear twister, white raksasa*

A battle cry echoed amidst the fighting.

Quinn frowned when a fifteen-year-old waif of a girl came flying over the deck of the ship. Axe clung to the rope with one hand and brandished her hatchet in the other. Blood splatter covered her youthful face as she swung, dropping slightly as she extended her arm—the blade sliding across an enemy's throat as she passed. She pumped the fisted weapon in the air, screaming "yahoooooooo" at the top of her lungs.

Quinn shook her head, pressing the notch on her staff for it to extend. The hidden compartment slid out, just as someone approached from behind. A hulking shadow loomed over her. She pivoted—swinging the blunt end up.

A masculine hand clamped down on the end as if anticipating her move.

"Myori's wrath," he cursed, stepping out of the shadows. Quinn quirked an eyebrow as Draeven said, "Watch what you're doing with that thing." Quinn rolled her eyes, swinging it back around to hit someone behind her without turning.

There was a grunt before a thump hit the deck.

"You were saying?" she replied, examining the newly pointed end of her staff, now gleaming with some fool's blood. She rather liked the look.

"Yeah, yeah—duck!" he shouted. She dropped to her knees just as his sword came from the side, cutting directly where her neck had just been. Another thump followed and Quinn grimaced.

"They're not going to stop," she yelled up to him as the fighting continued. Silver-haired men and women had descended upon their ship with an intent to kill, but they hadn't predicted the group that awaited them. She and Draeven worked in tandem cutting down soldiers. For everyone they managed to put down, another two took their place on deck. Axe swung back and forth, single-handedly decapitating the N'skari left and right. Quinn knew she was good with the hatchets, but she had to give it to her; Axe was better at protecting herself in a real fight than Quinn thought she would be. Still, the crew they'd brought was quickly dwindling and neither Lazarus, nor Vaughn or Dominicus were anywhere to be found.

"I don't understand why they're attacking us to begin with," Draeven shouted back, over the wind. She came and spun around, her attention sliding to the group of ships that surrounded them.

"Because Lazarus is an idiot," she muttered to herself. She glanced back at Draeven and the expression he was giving her said he heard it.

"What are you—" He broke off, side-stepping halfway around her to stab some other N'skari that had foolishly approached them with little to no stealth. The ship rocked harder, swaying danger-ously in the icy waters, making it difficult to balance as the waves churned unnaturally fierce for the clear skies.

Quinn narrowed her gaze on the horizon. *Could it be . . .*

"He sent a letter, but he never got a reply. The N'skari are attacking because we haven't been invited," she told him as water splashed the deck from the rough seas below.

"What?" he bellowed back, spinning her around so that her back touched his. "You've got to be—"

"Kidding?" she offered helpfully, twirling the staff to conk one person on the head and break another's neck with a hard blow. "We're under attack and surrounded from all sides. Do you have a better explanation?"

The only response she got was a growl. Bodies dropped around them as they slowly made their way toward the helm. Quinn peered over the side at the ship directly to their right. On the edge of the dock two women stood, their hands moving in carefully calculated movements. The blue light they gave off was undeniable.

Water weavers.

"*Potes*," she cursed. "Draeven, they're going to put us under. We need to find—" Her words broke off as she stared down the length of the ship. Lazarus stood there among the chaos, slowly beginning to unbutton his shirt, the dark swirls of his tattoos branded into his skin—*beneath* his flesh—becoming visible. Their gazes clashed, and in his expression she saw that he knew what the consequences of his impending actions would have.

Any chance of an alliance was already scarce, if he revealed what he was . . . Quinn shook her head and Lazarus stilled, paying more attention to her than to two approaching behind him. She made a snap decision.

"Quinn, what are you—" Draeven started, struggling to keep the horde at bay from taking command of the ship.

"Grab the helm," she told him.

"What? I'm a little busy—"

"I said grab the godsdamned helm!" she shouted, and in a quieter voice, she added, "I'm going to try something." Draeven dove out of the way to catch the spinning wood. He stopped it at the same moment she pivoted and pointed.

A wave of fear erupted from her veins, blasting through the line of attackers trying to make their way toward her. Screams echoed into the early morning as the sun started to rise. Quinn didn't block the light because she wanted them to see. All of them.

The group she'd attacked dropped to the floor,

their gazes unfocused, their bodies frozen in a catatonic state. It bought Quinn time to do the only thing she thought might be able to stop this before it was too late.

She lifted her staff in the air and shouted in N'skaran, "*Silence!*"

The soldiers on deck stilled. All heads twisted in her direction as Quinn grabbed onto their fear and held them fast. Even if they wanted to move, they wouldn't be able to.

"Who are you—" One of the men started in N'skaran.

"Quinn?" a woman called out in their language. "Quinn Darkova?" Several heads turned, including her own comrades. Quinn glanced down at her face, recalling a girl not much older than herself at the time. A girl born to a lower family and without any magical talent of her own. Quinn searched her memories for a name and murmured, "Isa LaFeirnn?"

The woman didn't smile, but a small amount of tension drained away. "It is you. We were told you'd been taken by slave traders. Your parents have been searching—"

"I've returned," she answered, cutting her off. "These people brought me back." She motioned to

Draeven, who was half-collapsed on the helm—then to Axe, who teetered on the edge of the railing, still gripping the rope in one hand. Her eyes were narrowed, shooting back and forth over all her potential targets. Lazarus stood with the guards behind him rooted to the ground by her own power. She didn't know where Vaughn or Dominicus were, but she hoped they'd made it their job to protect Lorraine.

The untrusting N'skari surveyed the area as they considered her words. Quinn remembered Isa being a kind girl. One that stood up for what was right, even if she was beaten into submission for it every time. She tried to walk the path true to the lighter gods. Quinn wondered if that was still the case. "If that is true, then we should welcome them for bringing you home."

"LaFeirnn." It was a single command, and Isa lowered her head in submission. Quinn grit her teeth because this voice was in her memory, too, and she didn't miss it. One of the men stepped forward. His long hair had been pulled back, and while over a decade had passed, Quinn recognized the thin, reedy-faced boy who had grown into a man that would make his family proud. The breath hissed between her teeth as he said, "Even if this is indeed the Darkova's missing child, how do we know it is the light that has guided her home?"

"I believe," Quinn started, "that while much time has gone by, it hasn't been long enough for N'skara to have changed so drastically." He frowned at her words and Quinn strode forward, stepping over the fallen soldiers on her way down the stairs. "My return would be a matter for the Council to discuss, as I am *highborn* by birthright." A murmur trickled over the deck, and in a voice only a shade lower, Quinn added, "If my parents have been searching for me, I am certain they would have prayed to Ramiel for justice. Now here I am, in the flesh, returned to them after all these years." Quinn shook her head, biting back the wicked grin threatening to break through. "If that's not the work of a god, I don't know what is, Edward."

"Yes, well," he paused, swallowing down whatever bitter words he knew he could not deliver. His eyes locked on hers and she met the coldness in kind. "It would seem that your return would be a miracle indeed if a god of the *light* has brought you here."

"Yes," she answered through a serpentine smile. "It would."

He shivered.

Quinn hadn't missed his underlying jabs. The prick was also higher born, but not so high as her. Even after ten years she outranked him in power, and he clearly despised it.

"If your desire is to return home, then we should take you ourselves and leave these" —he scrunched his nose in distaste— "*people* here."

Quinn rolled her eyes. "You've attacked their ship and killed half the crew manning it. I'm doubtful that neither Ramiel nor the goddess Telerah would show favor on that." She quirked an eyebrow and the glower he gave her could have burned holes through her skin were he capable of any real power. As it stood, she knew Edward to be a passion cleaver of little talent. While a strong one could have ripped away one's emotions or sense of self even, he would be capable of little more than dulling any particular feeling. Unlike the water weavers currently on standby to sink this ship should she let them take her and leave it. That wasn't an option.

"Ramiel would also understand that we attacked because an unknown vessel sailed into our territory. We had no idea if *they* intended harm," he replied icily.

"Perhaps." She nodded slowly. "But then I don't

make assumptions for what the gods do or don't believe. It would be unwise, should you assume wrong that is." She peered at the sky, holding for a moment before slowly letting her attention drift back to him. A dark gleam entered his gaze and a vicious thrill filled her. She did so love to play with her prey before she killed it.

"Very well," he answered after a moment. "If you wish to be given safe passage into Liph, I can arrange that. Your future, and theirs, will be in the hands of the Council once we reach the shores. I'm sure your parents will be anxious to see you after all this time."

"I'm sure they will," she agreed.

Very anxious, indeed.

N'skara

"Nothing is ever so simple as it seems. For it is the things left unspoken, unsaid, that illuminate the truth and its secrets."
— *Lazarus Fierté, soul eater, heir to Norcasta, observant warlord*

As fast as it had started, the fighting stopped.

Lazarus wasn't quite sure what to think of it. The way she cut men down and then spoke in that strange, terrible language as if she were *one of them*. He shook his head, his eyes raking down her form. While she might appear similar to them and talk like them, inside she was not like these people.

She was dark and twisted and cruel.

She was saevyana, whether he wanted her to be or not.

And right now, she was saving him his only chance at an alliance.

He'd been so close to removing his shirt and letting the N'skari suffer their fate. The ships around them would yield to the creatures beneath his skin, if he so willed it. But the people . . . they would not give him what he wanted if he forced it. No, an alliance would be out of the question as soon as he let his beasts loose upon the world. It wasn't his first choice, and if Quinn hadn't interceded, it would have been his only if he wanted them to make it out alive.

Lazarus glanced over. She spoke to the young male who'd defied her flippantly, condescension clearly coloring her voice, even if he didn't understand the words. The boy seemed to consider something, a darker shade entering his demeanor. Lazarus was only a second from stepping forward when he spoke. She smiled back, and it was all teeth.

The boy rounded and yelled something out to the ships beyond. The response that came back was again one that he couldn't understand. The silver-haired, pale-skinned people that had attacked now jumped from the deck. The N'skari entered the frigid waters without a thought or care, and moments later, all that remained was the boy and the girl that had spoken Quinn's name.

Her full name; the one he'd never heard before.

"Quinn," he said quietly. "A word?"

She stepped aside, murmuring something to the two in that language he didn't comprehend. Lazarus clenched his fists but didn't say anything to hurry her as he walked below deck. Dead bodies littered the planks, and fortunately for him, most of them weren't that of his crew.

He didn't hear her as she walked down the steps, following behind him, but he scented damp petals and fresh snow. Her soul was a lovely beacon of darkness amongst the light. It called to him, and he pivoted as she approached.

"Explain what's happening."

She quirked an eyebrow, crossing her arms over her chest as she leaned against the wooden wall. "You didn't listen to me and we were attacked for your misstep," she started, and he let out a growl.

"Right now, Quinn. I'm not a patient man, nor do I need to be scolded—"

She laughed derisively, the sound stopping him cold. "That's where you're wrong. What you did was stupid. Foolish. You like to scold me for reck-lessness but were I not a native, this would have ended poorly. You *owe me* for this, Lazarus."

He stood there, stunned by the frigidness in her voice.

"You are my v—"

"Vassal," she inserted. "Yes, I'm well aware of the terms of our contract. You dragged me over half the continent, blind to your plans, and now we're here—in a land where you don't know the language, you don't know the people, and I'd be shocked if you knew much about N'skara at all given your foolish attempt at an alliance." She raised both eyebrows, and the muscle in his jaw twitched.

He'd plucked her from the hovel she called a home and gave her a purpose; freedom beyond measure. He paid her well and he overlooked her violent outbursts. He gave her more than any other vassal in her place, because she was the key to everything. His kingdom. His crown.

Had he stolen her from her life? Yes. Had he manipulated and at times lied? Yes.

But he had a reason that outweighed anything.

It mattered more than any of her faults.

But she could also be his destruction. The end

to it all—should she not fall in line. He'd told himself that it would take time. That he would earn her loyalty. Her trust. Her respect.

Yet still, she defied him at every turn.

"I don't know what you think is going on here, Quinn, but I—"

"You're going to listen to me," she interrupted again. He opened his mouth to reply but she continued before he got the chance. "In this place, with these people, you are walking blind. I know what you desire, Lazarus, but if you have any hope of getting it—I need you to trust me this time."

He paused. The pounding in his head, the writhing of the souls; it made it difficult to keep his temper under control. That tenuous leash he held with Quinn was thinning, and not for the first time, he wondered who really held the power here, present circumstances aside.

But . . . she was asking for trust. The very thing he wanted from her. His past attempts to manipulate and coerce had gone horribly wrong. Perhaps trying a different approach would give him a different answer. If he truly wanted his crown, and put it above all—then even her infractions would have to wait to be punished.

"I'm willing to listen," he began. "However," he

held up a hand when she opened her mouth to interrupt him again. Leaning forward, he reached around and fisted her hair, tugging it back so that he could look at her, eye to eye. "You work for *me*. You are a member of *my* house. I don't care what color your skin is, because you are *mine*. You are not theirs. They do not get to keep you. Everything we do here is so that I can secure an alliance for my reign. Understood?"

Her crystalline eyes slanted as her gaze dropped to his lips. Just when he thought she was going to attempt to push him, to push this—whatever it was —she nodded once and stepped away. He let her go, the fine strands of her hair slipping through his fingers like silk.

"Trust me to do my part and you'll have your alliance in the end," she said. "And for the love of Forseya—don't give them a reason to kill you. Unlike Imogen, the N'skari don't give second chances."

The ship came to a gradual stop and someone yelled from the deck. Quinn sighed and turned on her heel, but just when he started to go after her, the door to his left opened.

"Did she just . . ." Dominicus started, pointing toward the stairs and trailing off at the expression on Lazarus' face. "I'm going to stay here guarding Lorraine," he said, wisely switching topics.

"You do that," Lazarus answered tersely. "Vaughn? Go guard Axe and make sure the child stays out of trouble." The mountain boy who had been cleaning blood off his blade nodded.

"I can handle little pirate."

Lazarus shook his head, running a hand down his face and exhaling deeply. Above deck, Quinn stood with Draeven already in tow. They waited with the two N'skari who had stayed on board. The male started to say something, but Quinn cut him off with a flippant dismissal.

Lazarus grinned to himself as they headed away and started down the ramp. He trailed behind, sidling up beside Draeven as they followed her.

The land of N'skara was a cold, desolate place. The docks were crafted from gray ashwood, and lined in rows along the shore. The beach itself was short, and mostly covered—but not all. Off to the far end where dangerous rocks jutted out, young boys and girls jumped into the treacherous waters and stayed below, only resurfacing when the harsh grate of a woman's voice rang out.

"The rumors didn't do it justice," Draeven murmured. "I can't imagine Quinn living here."

They looked out into the freezing waters. Tiny islands broke up the surface, scattered throughout. On land, men and women worked in robes of gray —their talk oddly silent for a shipyard. Out beyond the ashwood planks the land rose up into hills that led to the Cisean mountains beyond. Buildings made of plaster and stone were stacked on top of each other, row by row.

Lazarus shook his head.

"There's a reason she left," he said. It occurred to him that despite the odd comment and vague mentions, he still didn't know that reason. Nor did he know where she sat with these people that had once been her own. However, judging by the stiffness in her shoulders and brass knuckles she kept on her hands despite the battle having ended—he knew that not all was as it seemed.

She might have stopped them from attacking and convinced the N'skari to bring them here, but she was still on edge. Anxious. Her magic left blackened footprints everywhere she walked. Not anyone else could see them. Those soot-colored imprints left behind leaked into the air, giving him a slight taste of her magic, and hostility pounded through him. The emotion was not his own.

They stepped onto the cobbled streets. Seashells

of the lightest pinks and off-white had been crushed and mixed in with mortar to create the walkways. N'skari children stopped and stared, but with a sharp jerk from the boy's head that led them, parents grabbed their slender arms and pulled them along. There was no screaming or crying of infants, just as there had been no shouting along the docks. If not for the people, largely robed in swaths of gray, Lazarus might have thought it abandoned. It wasn't empty, though; merely silent apart from the hushed whispers that followed them. They passed a bridge overhead that spanned from one building to another, forming an arch as they entered a courtyard.

Statues of marble rose up in a semi-circle around the base of stairs that rose as tall as any building. Columns of white peeked out over the edge of the elevated platform.

Quinn walked by the statues without even a glance and started to scale the stairs. He and Draeven moved to follow after her when two guards stepped out from behind the marble figures, the spears they held in hand crossing to block entrance.

"What is the meaning of this?" Lazarus asked loudly, being sure his voice carried. Stone-faced as the buildings around them, the guards said nothing, though Quinn paused and looked back. She spoke in low tones to the boy and girl beside her. Again, the boy answered.

"I'm to go before the Council and plead our case," she called down to him.

"Then we are as well," he answered. Her gaze grew hard, but Lazarus wasn't yielding. "I trust you, but I do not trust them. Either these guards step aside, or I go through them. It is their decision." She sighed and shook her head, but spoke to the boy.

Lazarus saw him stiffen and then glance back. They argued for a moment, Quinn motioning to him and then just as before, the guards decided to stand down—without a command from the boy. Lazarus narrowed his eyes, slowly stalking through the gap between the statue of Ramiel, God of Balance and Justice, and Skadi, Goddess of the Winter. He felt as if their unseeing eyes were following him as he began to climb the stairs. Beside him, Draeven huffed, "I'm beginning to hate this place already." Lazarus knew his comment had little to do with the stairs and more to do with the cold fixation of the boy that stared at them.

The N'skari made a comment under his breath and Quinn bristled, her left hand tightening as though she were going to take a swing. Muscles taut under the tension, she turned and gave all of them the cold shoulder as she hiked up the rest of the stairs, not losing her pacing, even toward the top.

They trailed after her, and all the while a sense of dread was beginning to thicken in his stomach as if stones of lead were weighing it down. He swallowed hard, pushing his anticipation aside as he finally reached the top. His boots came down on a flat block of marble, likely cut from the same source as the statues below. Across its gleaming surface, Quinn stood at the base of a temple so great in its grandeur that even Lazarus had to take a moment to peer up at the sloping roofs and the crown molding that surrounded the pillars, through the stained glass windows on a set of double doors that had been cracked ajar, all the way to the people that stood between them.

In front of Quinn, a man and woman waited, and while all the N'skari looked similar—the resemblance between the woman and Quinn was too striking to be anything other than familial.

"Do you think those are her parents?" Draeven asked, beside him. Neither man moved as Quinn stood, her body language lukewarm at best. Her expression unmoved for what one would expect of a girl reunited with her parents, but it was not her body that gave away the truth.

"I do," Lazarus said. Her father's gaze was not emotionless, but it was cold. Joyless and apathetic. If there had ever been any warmth inside of her, it would have shivered and died in the presence of such a man.

"I wonder why they never searched for her when she was a slave," Draeven whispered, his voice trailing off as neither party made any move to embrace.

For the first time, Lazarus was beginning to wonder that as well, because the expressions on their faces were not that of parents happy to be reunited with their child . . .

It was that of guilt and fear.

It was the look of people who had something to *hide*.

A Bitter Reunion

"Be wary of those abandoned. You never know which of your mistakes may come back to haunt you."
— *Quinn Darkova, vassal of House Fierté, fear twister, white raksasa*

The chill of the ice beneath her boots was incomparable to the frigid gaze of Percinius and Ethel Darkova. With their silver hair and crystalline eyes, they were practically identical to Quinn's own coloring. Except Quinn had changed in the years she'd been away.

The child they'd rejected and left to the greedy

hands of slave traders was gone; in her place stood a woman who had survived many hardships.

Her hair was no longer the color of fresh snow and her skin now bore the scars of years honing her defiance. The black sheep of the Darkova line and her parents' own personal shame had come back from the dead, and it was clear that they were not pleased.

Quinn felt a delightfully wicked smile spread across her lips. Not by one brow quirk did they reveal their shock at her presence. No, instead, Quinn's father merely frowned and reached out, clasping her by the arm and drawing her out of the entrance, away from the temple that housed the Council's chambers and toward the side of the building.

Quinn waited for an appropriate amount of time to pass as her father dragged her to the side before she quickly and firmly removed his limb from her own.

"Father." Quinn's eyes were chips of ice as they met Percinius' gaze.

He sucked in a breath, as if the reminder of his relation to her offended him, but before he could speak, Quinn nodded for Lazarus and Draeven to continue just inside the temple. Lazarus' focus slid from her to her parents before returning to Quinn. She merely shook her head and motioned for him to go. His lips thinned and his jaw clenched, but with a sharp nod and another dark glare toward her parents, he and Draeven disappeared inside.

When Quinn faced them once more, she could see the slight tick in her father's jaw that belied his rage. He wasn't used to being ignored, even for the brief moment it took Quinn to make sure Lazarus and the others weren't nearby. She raised an eyebrow at him.

Ethel was the first to speak, her words sharp and curt. "What are you doing here?"

Quinn turned her attention to her mother, glaring down at the shorter woman. "I'm here as a vassal for Lord Lazarus Fierté of Norcasta," she replied.

"You may take your *master*," Percinius spat the intolerable word, "and return from whence you came."

Quinn's lips pressed together; one hand clenched—but she couldn't act on their words. Not here. Not now. She'd coached herself through what those first words would be a hundred times over, but nothing compared to actually doing it.

She stepped closer and something in her expression must have warned them of her desires—or perhaps they recognized the darkness that had only grown in those long and lonely years—because they each took a step back. Quinn halted and a true smile blossomed across her face, as lovely as it was terrible.

"You are mistaken, *Father*." Percinius narrowed his eyes at her. He truly hated that title, especially as it came from her lips. "He is not my master, as you put it. I'm not his pet. I'm not a slave at all. I'm a vassal of House Fierté and I have the freedom to come and go as I please."

"Whatever house he comes from has no power here," Ethel snapped, her distaste clear as she reached out and gripped her husband's arm. Her attention dropped to Quinn's own arm. It was obvious she wanted to reach out and touch her daughter, but not for the same reasons other mothers might. As a semi-powerful trust spinner, Ethel needed only to touch someone to get them to trust her enough to reveal all of their secrets. Quinn knew that the strength of a trust spinner's abilities were only effective on those with less power than themselves.

If she touched her, Quinn wouldn't say a word.

Ethel, however, likely wouldn't fare so well against her own bare skin.

Fear was a terrible thing, and she feared her daughter greatly.

"I'm here as a translator and a mediator. Whether or not his house has any power is unimportant. It would benefit the N'skari not to kill him. Unless you expect to win a war against three countries," Quinn finally said after enough silence had passed. Ethel Darkova blinked.

"What do you mean?" Percinius demanded.

"Lazarus Fierté is the next king of Norcasta, and thus far he has gained an alliance with the Barbarian King of the Ciseans and the Pirate Queen of Ilvas. Were anything to happen to him here . . ." She let the sentence trail away as she admired the way what little color her parents had drained away.

"That's impossible," Percinius spluttered. "Such an alliance has never existed."

"You also never expected my return, yet here I stand before you," Quinn said tartly. Her mother's mouth slipped ajar in shock and outrage. She sighed and let her smile drop away as she stepped back.

Her parents had seemed so large to her as a

child. So powerful. So . . . god-like. But the gods were gods, not men among them; certainly not these two before her. While her mother had been beautiful in youth, the lines of her age were beginning to show. Harsh and severe as the paddle she loved to use when Quinn was but a child. Her father had always seemed tall and imposing, but he was a dwarf of a man compared to Lazarus. His silver hair had become thin and his stomach stouter.

No, they weren't gods. Just depraved people hiding beneath their white-robed facade.

"As enticing as this reunion is," Quinn started, backing away, "I'm expected before the Council."

Percinius was the first to gather his composure. "They'll ensure that you and your primitive horde are sent back, if not executed," he said as he glared at her.

Quinn sent him a bored, disinterested look. "I'm sure they won't act too harshly," she said, "particularly since you'll be vouching for me."

Ethel blinked again as Percinius' gaze narrowed into thin slits. "Why would we do that? You are unwelcome here. No matter the lord you travel with. You don't belong in N'skara."

Quinn took a deep breath, but those words

didn't sting the same as they had when she'd been only thirteen and had chains placed around her wrists and ankles for the first time. She'd held those words close to her heart, every night as the ship that carried her sailed further and further from her homeland, the only place she'd ever known. And her heart hardened. It became as cold and frigid as the frost-covered ground and when the slave traders landed, Quinn was not a Darkova anymore, because Quinn Darkova was dead.

Her parents sold her, but it was those words that killed her.

She'd told them to herself a thousand times over, and it seemed that thousand was enough because they didn't sting anymore. Quinn had grown too cold to feel the bite.

"You will support my requests," she said slowly. "Because the faster my lord completes his mission here, the more expedient my departure will be." She didn't give them room to reply. To object. "That is, unless you'd like for me to tell them how I became a slave to begin with . . ." Quinn let that threat hang for a moment, the clarity on her parents' faces making it obvious that they knew her disappearance from N'skara would only be a single mark in a list of infractions they'd committed.

Percinius' mouth shut, his lips forming a line as he stared at her with revulsion. Ethel wasn't much better, except she at least had the graces to turn her face to the ground while her guilt ate at her.

"They won't believe you," Percinius said. There was a fire there. He wanted to fight.

He didn't realize he'd already lost. She survived and came for them.

"Perhaps," she mused. "Not all will, but the lower born might, and the higher born—let's just say your name will be dragged through every dirty little secret you thought you could hide. I'll bring them into the light and show everyone who the Darkovas really are . . . and once the accusation is made, all it would take is a trust spinner equal or greater in power than mother and poof" —she snapped her fingers—"you're both ruined. Disgraced. You'd be lucky if the N'skari only banished you instead of drowning you in the ocean as an offering to Ramiel." She tilted her head and with a slight shrug to her shoulders said, "You'll support my bid for an alliance and anything else I ask for—or I'll show you the maruda you believe me to be."

"Percinius, we—" Ethel started.

He shushed his wife with a single scowl and

then spun back to his daughter. Quinn didn't need to say more. She had them—because the one thing she could always count on her parents for was to care about their reputation more than anything or anyone.

"This was a lovely chat." She reached forward and patted Percinius' arm, causing him to stiffen as she moved to leave. "Thank you for the welcome home."

Quinn pivoted toward the temple's entrance and straightened her shoulders as she marched away, feeling their gazes upon her back. Just inside, Lazarus and Draeven stood waiting. As she approached, Draeven's eyebrows rose in question. Quinn shook her head slightly and strode past.

They fell in line behind her, trailing after as she moved farther into the temple—past the towers that marked the end of the antechamber and the beginning of the interior corridor. Quinn continued past the smaller pillars as they grew in size until she was all the way into the chancel and before the rounded perches of the Council members.

She faced the six pedestals for each of the highborn families that sat upon the Council, many of them already filled with the heads of each house. They stared down at her from beyond their wall of pillars. A seventh figure, the tribe's elder, sat at the very center of the half circle, performing the same slow perusal. Quinn hadn't seen the old man since before she'd left N'skara, but he'd hardly changed. Udolf Emsworth appeared as fossilized as he always had been.

Ancient, age-spotted, thin knuckly fingers curled around the edge of the largest pillar from which the elder council member rested. "Quinn Darkova." He spoke in a voice that was as deep as it was raspy. "For over ten years we feared your existence snuffed out by the greed and immorality beyond the protection of our boundaries, but on this day, you have returned. We welcome our child back into our arms and thank your"—the elder gave a slight pause, his clouded gray-blue eyes sliding to the side over Lazarus and Draeven's presence before he continued—"friends for their roles in bringing you back to us."

Quinn stepped forward and met the elder's expectant stare. Letting the lilting tonality of her mother tongue roll from her lips, she spoke. "My greatest appreciation for your welcome, Elder Emsworth," she said. "We've traveled a long way and look forward to a long-deserved rest in Liph."

The Elder's brows furrowed, and his focus

shifted to just beyond Quinn's shoulder again. "It seems your time away has addled your memory, dear Darkova," an unwelcome voice said. Edward's face peered back at her from his own pedestal. "We do not allow outsiders to stay beyond the fall of night. Your *companions*," he hissed the word, "may rest upon their ship as it sails back to wherever it came from."

Quinn cursed her inattention. This was why the man had acquiesced to her requests so easily—why he had agreed to bring them back so readily. He was on the bloody council and had probably taken the seat from his own father, despite his feeble power as a Maji. Quinn scowled at his triumphant smirk.

"I assure you, my memory remains unaffected," Quinn said tersely, "and *I* will be resting wherever *they* rest."

A council woman with her hair pulled back in a tight bun scoffed. Quinn examined her, the silver medallion upon her breast proclaiming her to be from the Zandeas line. "That's preposterous," she said. "It is your duty to return to your household and—"

"I'm afraid there's been a miscommunication," Quinn interrupted. "I'm not here to be returned to my people." At that, several of the Council members began to mutter to themselves and shift around uncomfortably upon their perches. At the edge of her vision, Quinn noted that Percinius and Ethel had taken their seats upon the pedestal meant for the Darkova line. "I have come back to facilitate an alliance between N'skara and the future king of Norcasta."

The murmurings became abruptly louder. Behind her, Lazarus and Draeven exchanged a quick glance before stepping forward as if sensing —rather than comprehending—what her words meant. Lazarus opened his mouth, but before he could speak, the Elder lifted a hand and halted the series of harsh and impassioned whispers from the rest of the Council.

"There has never been an alliance between the N'skari and another country, Quinn, and I highly doubt there will be now," the Elder said. "We are grateful to your companions for their cooperation in bringing you back, but—"

"They did not bring me back," Quinn corrected him, once again interrupting and eliciting an outraged squawk from one of the other council members at the disrespect. She ignored it. "I am here to translate for Lazarus Fierté, the chosen heir to the Norcastan throne. That is all." With a pause to survey the Elder's reaction as well as those around him, she released her next statement. One guaranteed to send them all spiraling into a state of disorganized bewilderment. "I have chosen not to return to N'skara."

Voices rose above murmurs and mutterings almost immediately.

"Unbelievable—"

"Outrageous—"

"Elder Emsworth, you must do something—"

"Such disrespect—"

Quinn met and held the old man's stare with confidence. His eyes narrowed upon her as she remained patient in awaiting his response. The wrinkled fingers that curled around the edge of his pillar disappeared for a moment as he raised his fist into the air and brought it down upon the surface of the perch on which he sat. The echoing sound of his strike froze all other exclamations. Every eye in the room turned to Udolf Emsworth.

"Quinn Darkova, second heir to the Darkova line." The Elder's voice deepened as he spoke, vibrating in baser tones throughout the room. "You are N'skari by blood and Maji by birth. Your place is with the tribe."

"My lineage is irrelevant," she said, forcing back her irritation as once again her words caused a tirade of impassioned replies, each growing louder than the next. "My place," Quinn continued, "is wherever *I* decide it is, and currently, I've decided that it's with Lazarus Fierté."

Shocked silence met her words.

"By the grace of Leviticus . . ." someone whispered, breaking the spell that had suddenly fallen over them. "You've truly lost your mind."

"Quinn?" Lazarus' voice was restrained as he called her name. She glanced back at him over her shoulder and shook her head. Without another word, he nodded and stepped back as she faced the Council once more.

Quinn tilted her chin ever so slightly, eyeing her parents. Percinius Darkova's face appeared pained as he sat forward. Ethel was stone-faced as she sat with her spine parallel to the wall at her back, her focus on somewhere much further away than the goings on within the temple chambers. Quinn's lips quirked at that. Her mother never could stand much for the stress of reality.

"A proposal for the Council," Percinius announced, his words stilted as though someone were forcibly pulling them from his mouth. Quinn supposed in a sense she was. "We allow the foreigners three nights within Liph."

Quinn waited for more. She knew three nights would do nothing to proceed with Lazarus' intentions, but it seemed that her father could only push himself so far. He was as unable as he was unwilling to suggest anything beyond that—not even a proposal to hear Lazarus speak. Her jaw hardened as she gritted her teeth.

"Two weeks," Quinn replied, focusing her attention on the Elder. He, after all, had far more weight upon the Council than any other singular family. "Give them two weeks to—"

"Unacceptable," the Zandeas woman cried just as Elder Emsworth held up his hand once more.

"*If*," Elder Emsworth said, gaining Quinn's full attention, "we allow your companions to stay, you will consider remaining when they leave?" he asked.

Quinn would have rather walked straight into the bowels of Mazzulah's realm, to the darkest depths of the most depraved sections of the god's wretched inferno before she contemplated remaining within N'skara. But not by a single movement or twitch of her expression did she betray those feelings. She merely stared at the Elder.

"Would you allow my lord and his vassals two

weeks and an audience with the Council?" she asked.

He was shaking his head before Quinn even finished. "Three nights and an audience," he offered in return.

"Elder Emsworth." Quinn kept her voice even, polite, and as mannered as she could stomach. "Three nights is not enough. The ship's crew must rest and replenish their supplies for the journey back as well."

The elder leaned back and remained quiet. As much as she loathed to admit it, Quinn realized that she would not get two weeks. It had been a feat, thus far, that the elder was even contemplating allowing Lazarus an audience—though she knew it was merely to humor her. Quinn sucked in a breath as she considered her next words. She had no flowery sayings that would win them over, but this was a battle that could not be won by brashness and anger. She needed to know when to press forward and when to retreat.

With clenched fists, Quinn realized that now was not the time to press forward. Though it pained her and went against every fiber of her being, when next she spoke, it was to offer a compromise.

"Ten days," she finally said. "My companions

and I will remain within Liph for ten days, and Lazarus Fierté will be granted an audience with the Council and consideration for an alliance."

The room held its collective breath as Elder Emsworth leaned forward. "We allow you this, Quinn Darkova," he began, "and regardless of the decisions made in the audience granted, you will consider staying when they leave?"

Quinn didn't blanch, though her desire to do so was great. She held her tongue, deliberating on her answer. She didn't want to outright lie. They wouldn't believe it if she did. She had to choose her words carefully. Quinn pivoted, observing the room and the faces surrounding her. Many of the Council members were austere and rigid, compliant with the elder, but obviously untrusting of her. The older chairs, she knew, were aware of her own power. The younger chairs—such as Edward—merely scowled at her as they kept their mouths sealed out of respect and deference to Udolf Emsworth.

"I can guarantee you, Elder Emsworth," Quinn replied, choosing her words as delicately as she would select a weapon to kill with. "I will give a future in N'skara my utmost consideration as I think of my family and the memories I have of my home country." She would allow the reminders of her past to finally seep up from where she had buried them long ago. She would let them guide her to do what she had come back to do even as she kept her promise to Lazarus as faithfully as she could. "You will allow us ten days and an audience with the Council to discuss an alliance," she said, "and when the time comes for my companions to leave, you will have your answer."

Udolf Emsworth straightened upon his pedestal, and with a ringing baritone, announced, "You are granted ten days within the sanctuary of Liph, and granted an audience in three days' time, upon the midday sun."

Quinn nodded and bowed her head in respect. At her back, Draeven and Lazarus followed her lead and bowed their heads as well. Council members began to murmur, many of their voices sullen as they began to descend from their pillars. Quinn kept her focus on the floor until the elder had dismounted from his position and gone from the chamber. When she again lifted her head, it was to catch sight of her parents. From the expressions on their cool, icy faces, she knew they were silently trying to figure out what her next move would be.

Quinn smiled. They would know soon enough.

The Night is Home

"The night is home to creatures like us—it provides the cover
for the secrets we hide."
— *Lazarus Fierté, soul eater, heir to Norcasta, stalker*
warlord

Liph was not white so much as it was a somber, wintry gray. In the daylight, Lazarus had noted that the ice and snow made the structures and bridges and roadways appear prominent, but in the dusk and beyond, it became a veritable blanket of muted moonlight—a cerulean layer of frost through which to view the N'skari people and their lives.

"Your room." Lazarus pulled his attention away from the windows to face their current host who spoke to them in hard monosyllabic words that sounded awkward, though they were Norcastan. Their host—a relative of one of the Council member's that was allowing them the use of his second home—was unused to the more guttural sounding language.

"Thank—" The door shut halfway through Draeven's halfhearted 'thank you' and he huffed. "Prickly bunch, aren't they?"

"They do seem to be rather fractious," Lazarus agreed absently as he returned his focus to the window.

"I see where Quinn gets her phenomenal personality," Draeven said drily as he crossed the room and began to search through drawers and night tables of either bed with distracted curiosity.

Just outside, fires were being lit down the street —singular dots of yellow in the dark meant to guide those still milling about. The chill of the night seeped in through the walls, settling into Lazarus' bones as he observed the surroundings beyond the glass. He was growing to realize the weather was not the coldest thing about this place.

He'd been unable to understand the majority of

the conversation between Quinn and the members of the N'skari Council, but he saw the way their eyes followed her. Some wary, others curious, but beneath both, there was a sense of unrest. She may have spoken their language, she may have understood their customs, but as the meeting had droned on, Lazarus became all the more certain that Quinn was not one of them.

There was a sense of relief in that, but also a pervasive concern. It was clear that the N'skari trusted her no more than they trusted him. Why that was, however, he could only guess.

Pacing away from the window, Lazarus strode the length of the room.

"Do you think the others are bunking together as well?" Draeven asked as he gave up his snooping and flopped onto the nearest bed.

"I believe so," Lazarus replied absently. Draeven observed him for a moment before sitting up on the bed, moving so that he was perched on the edge.

"Did you find it strange how they treated her?" he asked. Lazarus paused and met his left-hand's pointed stare. Draeven didn't wait for his master to reply. "I have the feeling that there are mixed opinions about her return."

"They fear her," Lazarus said.

"Yes." Draeven nodded, arching up from the bed and moving toward the windows. "But there has to be more to it, don't you think?" With night falling, shadows and stone and trees all blended together in darker shades of gray. Lazarus met Draeven's stare as it scrutinized him through their reflections on the window. Like him, Draeven saw more than he was saying.

Lazarus reached up and scrubbed a hand down the side of his jaw.

"She's still hiding things from me," he muttered darkly. He despised the truth of his words to the core of his very being. He had chosen to trust her and still she defied him with her latent words.

Across the room, Draeven snorted. "I'll say," he replied, his focus fastened on whatever held his attention beyond the window.

"I don't believe that she'll betray me," Lazarus continued. "She can't. Her contract won't allow it."

"I suppose there's nothing to worry about then," Draeven shot back.

Lazarus glared at his left-hand. She couldn't betray him outright, but she could mislead him. He'd given her room to accomplish her task and it occurred to him that he might grow to regret that.

But Quinn was not a creature to be caged. She was not a beast he had hoped to tame. No. He needed to give her room, or she'd rip everything he was trying to build to shreds.

With a slow inhale, Lazarus approached a bed and sat heavily upon it. "I'll speak with her in the morning," he finally decided. He would reaffirm her loyalty and ensure that his will was taking precedence . . . *for now.*

"If she's still here in the morning," Draeven said, lifting his head as Lazarus' brow furrowed. Draeven pointed to the window. "I believe your little fear twister is doing some clandestine skulking."

Lazarus' legs carried him from the bed to the window with a speed and force that belied his earlier decision. True enough, a figure in a dark cloak was striding across the street. Halfway over the cobbles, the hood was brushed back by a wayward wind and soft strands of purple-silver hair escaped. Feminine fingers grasped the hood and jerked it back up as the figure hurried along, disappearing between two buildings directly across from them.

Cursing under his breath, Lazarus turned and stalked to the door. "I'll just stay here and keep the beds warm, then, shall I?" Draeven called behind him.

"Alert the others if I do not return by sunrise."

Lazarus continued for the door; the whole of his attentions focused solely on the fear twister that had slipped through his fingers. Snatching a cloak from an emptied room on his way down, he let himself out into the night—pulling the fabric up to hide his features much in the way he'd witnessed Quinn doing the same. It was little defense against the biting cold, but Lazarus' own irritation was fuel enough for the march.

He followed the path she'd taken, sliding between the two buildings and heading down the street. Even though lamps had been lit, the streets of Liph were empty. It was vastly different from Tritol, which would have been overcrowded with drunkards and street musicians by this time—and even Cisea, which held feasts that lasted well into the early morning.

In N'skara, though, they weren't welcome and there were no celebrations to be had.

Quinn's magical signature, footprints black as pitch, guided Lazarus through the freshly fallen snow. He wondered if she realized that she did it. If she noticed how, even now, magic leaked from her everywhere she went, guiding him as nothing else could. He inhaled that scent of damp petals with the bitter crisp of winter, and his pulse thrummed, the beats of his heart deepening. He tracked her to the front of a wealthier home several streets away from their own accommodations.

Quinn stood before a large arching door of blackwood with polished silver finishes. She paused and he tilted his head, watching her from down the street. She waited several minutes, muttering to herself too softly for the wind to carry. She pulled her shoulders back and inhaled deeply, before raising her fist and letting it thump twice upon the door. A moment passed, and then two, but just when he thought there would be no answer, the door creaked open, light spilling into the street.

He couldn't see whoever was there, but Quinn's face had become completely unreadable. Her features were hard as the marbled statues around her, the set of her lips thin as if she were holding herself back from something.

A series of harsh mutterings were spoken before she went through the doorway and the blackwood slammed shut behind her. Lazarus grimaced, tilting his face up and examining the three storied building and over the wrought iron gate that wrapped around the side of the house. Lazarus narrowed his eyes, unsure whether it was there to keep the likes of him out or if it was meant to keep secrets in.

With a heavy exhale, he decided it was likely both and that it wouldn't stop him.

Pulling on the soul of the wraith beneath his skin, he used the madness of a rage thief gone rogue to cover him in shadows as he strode for the gate. There was no lock, no latch, no opening. It didn't matter.

Lazarus reached up and grasped the heavy metal in both fists, using his strength to lift himself off the ground and clear over the metal spikes. As he dropped toward the ground, he felt a slight resistance, followed by a tear. He glanced back at the wad of black fabric mounted on a spike, whipping back and forth in the frozen wind like a flag of death.

Lazarus sighed, his attention dropping to the ragged tear in his cloak from the waist below. Two skinny strips of black barely touched his boots. The rest of it hanging on the iron gate. He plucked the fabric from the barb and turned to survey the side of the building. Straight up with no real handholds or ways to climb, he resorted to walking down the side. Grass couldn't grow here in this frozen wasteland, but trees did, and the twigs that resulted snapped underfoot as he trekked the length of the house, pausing around back.

Voices drifted over him, familiar, though he couldn't understand the words. He slowly rounded the corner, pulling on the wraith's soul and manipulating the shadows to conceal him.

Light spewed forth from a window and he moved to stand before it in the quickly darkening night. Standing not three feet from the pane, Lazarus peered in.

His blood heated. His pulse quickened.

What was she doing with them?

Twisted Memories

"For every bit that Lady Fortune is fickle, his Lord Ramiel is just—but never merciful."
— *Quinn Darkova, vassal of House Fierté, fear twister, white raksasa*

I ce nipped at her bare hands but she hardly noticed. Once upon a time the cold was painful. It made her burn from the inside out. It suffocated her. Confined her. Until the day she was sold like a common whore. Quinn stopped before her childhood home. The pale walls were ghostly in the night's light, but there would be no whispers from the dead. No. Everything that went on in this wretched place stayed here.

She paused, the memories assaulting her like a physical blow. Images of her youth flashed before her. Glimpses of little silver-haired girls and white robes stained red. Echoes from the shouting followed her still. A chill ran up her spine as the day it all came to an end pushed forward in her mind. She stalled, letting those last moments wash over her once more.

Reliving the pain because the hurt kept her cold. So cold she burned, but as she'd learned that day—some things were worse than the cold.

Quinn had been hiding for days. Her last outburst had changed things. She'd known it in her bones as surely as she knew the sun would set. Her mother had been quiet in her presence every time they spoke. Her words stilted. Stiff. She avoided her father entirely every chance she got. He often stayed late at temple or meeting with the Council, and that made it easier.

Simpler.

She stayed in her room as much as she could. Keeping anyone and everyone away. Not that anyone was coming to see her after she did what she did.

Quinn had always been strong. Her magic the purest and also the vilest in all her family. It was their secret. Their shame. She'd been seeing the dark wisps as long as she could remember, but lately it was more than that. She smelled them. She felt them. They called to her like a babe did its mother. In the dark when she was alone, she liked to play with them because they didn't judge her. They didn't hate. They didn't throw rocks at her or threaten to drown her in the ocean for her black magic.

She'd heard what other Maji's magic was like. That they needed to reach for it and the power of the gods would be bestowed on them to do great things. Quinn never had to reach for hers, though. In moments of pain it came to her, seeking her out, giving her comfort as nothing else would.

That's what it had done that day.

She didn't realize that in her comfort, other people would hurt. She didn't know it caused pain like no other.

She just wanted her own torment to stop—but then the screaming started.

So, in her room she stayed, because there she was safe. Alone. She couldn't hurt anyone nor be hurt. She had the wisps for company, and while it saddened her for the friend she had to keep away, it was better than the alternative.

Her tiny hand curled and uncurled. The black strands rising. Twining. They slithered over her skin and the hairs on her arm rose in response. A chill crept up her spine as she sensed dread coming from downstairs. Quinn lifted her head and stared at the door, debating whether she should venture out.

The choice was made for her.

"Quinn," her father called. His voice was not soft, but it wasn't hard either. That chill crept higher, the hairs on her neck tingling. Even as a girl no older than thirteen, she knew when she should worry. "Come down for dinner, Daughter."

She swallowed hard. To refuse his order would incur his wrath. Her gaze trailed over the wood paneled floors and toward the long branch of ashwood in the corner of her room. There was nothing next to it. Nothing on it. The singular branch was near two inches thick and four feet long.

And when she disobeyed an order . . .

Quinn swallowed again. She took her beatings in silence and kept her head held high, but just this once she didn't want to. She didn't want to test the boundaries because she'd pushed them too far already. Broke them. Shattered them.

She was scared that those splintered pieces would cut her should she get too close to it again, and that when she bled, she might not stop.

Quinn pushed her legs over the edge of her bed. Her feet were bare and the floor cold to the touch, but she hardly noticed it at the time. Her pale arms wrapped around herself as she went to her door and twisted the handle. It swung open and the only thing that carried up the stairs was fear.

She felt it in her veins as she took every silent step toward the stairwell. She pushed it down, despite her gut telling her she was going the wrong way. That she should run. Quinn did what every good daughter did, and she listened to her father.

But when she reached the end of the stairwell, it was not her father waiting for her.

"Who are—"

The words she was asking didn't even register before they tugged at her arms. Three burly men, stinking like fermented ale and day-old piss, surrounded her. The black tendrils leapt to her defense. They tried to protect her, but unlike her family, she didn't know how to use her magic. She was never taught. Only shamed. Only shunned.

The black magic in her veins tried to stop them, but ultimately it failed.

Manacles were placed on her wrists. The stone on them glowed red.

When that couldn't contain her dark power, they tried for her legs, and a true panic consumed. "Stop," she screamed. "Please!"

They didn't stop as they grabbed both of her arms. One of the men crumpled to his knees. Through gritted teeth, he said, "Hurry."

The third man did. He crouched down. Larger, more menacing chains in his hands. Over his head she saw them. Her mother and father.

"Mother," she called out. "Please don't let them take me. Please—I promise I'll be good. I promise!" She screamed at the first touch of iron against her ankle. It was a feeling she would become well acquainted with. The second man holding her dropped to his knees as well. The breath hissed between his teeth as the tendrils went after him. Like a rabid dog loyal only to its master, they laid into him with a ferocity that not even power-stripping manacles could contain.

"You brought this on yourself," her mother said.

"I'm sorry," she cried. Quinn's eyes watered. "I didn't mean to hurt her. I just wanted it to stop. I just got so angry when she told me about—" Iron wrapped around her other ankle and the tendrils dispersed. Like smoke in the air they drifted off and she couldn't catch them. Her only friend in the darkness was gone.

She reached for the power inside her, but something was stopping her.

A wall so thick, so tall, she couldn't go around it —her power was caged.

She couldn't hold back the sob as they placed one more manacle on her. Iron two inches thick wrapped around her throat. The lock clicked and the metal scraped as the man in front of her stood. She'd never forget his eyes. They were blue, like her own; like her families—like N'skara.

Blue as the ocean. Blue as the ice. Blue like sin.

People thought that black was the color of corruption, but they were wrong.

All things corrupt in the world were tinged with blue.

He lifted the chain and yanked once. She fell to her knees on the white marble.

"Thank you," her father said. "Now as promised . . ."

She felt the first blow the hardest. Through watery vision she looked up at him.

Percinius Darkova. Her father. The man that had raised her.

"Why?" It was the only thing she would get to ask, as the next blow struck her mouth and she tasted blood.

"You're vile," he said. His fist struck again.

"Evil," he continued. Again.

"Twisted." Again.

Over and over he hit her. The punches blurred together. So did the blood. Snot ran down her face and she'd stopped crying somewhere along the way.

"Hey now—" one of the men said. "You sold her, and we promised you your kicks because it makes them more compliant in the long run, but we need to keep her alive."

The punches stopped, but the pain didn't. Her stomach ached deeply. Breathing sent sharp pains into her sides. Every part of her face hurt. She couldn't see out her left eye. She could only make out distorted images on her right. The slavers that took her had to carry her after that. They smuggled her onto a ship and dumped her in the cargo hold.

It was only in the coming days that she'd learn why her father had been in so many Council meeting those last days. The slavers had been invited ashore by her parents, and though the Council denied them the right to sell, they got what they came for.

An N'skari fear twister too young to know the power she held.

A child that for the first time in her life was completely and utterly powerless.

She learned in the coming weeks the blessing that was the cold. The power to be numb, to be silent, to be as unforgiving as the winter she'd known her whole life.

That cold inside is what kept her alive. The burn it created is what kept her going.

And now, she'd returned to finish what they started.

Quinn strode up the front steps to the door. The last time she'd seen this door was over the shoulder of a stranger as he carried her away in the dead of night. Today she came back of her own volition.

Quinn took a deep breath, knowing that at least she was ready.

Then she lifted her hand and knocked twice.

The Dark Inside

*"Even the damned once had the innocence of a babe, just as
the good hold a seed of darkness in them too."*
*— Quinn Darkova, vassal of House Fierté, fear twister,
white raksasa, second daughter of the Darkova Household*

Quinn trailed the tips of her fingers over the straight-back lounge her mother always entertained from. The fireplace roared nearly as loud as the wind, but that was a distant thing compared to the subtle rage that pounded through her veins. She no longer had a heated anger toward her parents; that fire had died long ago. Instead it was the ashy remains that froze over that plagued her now. An anger so cold, a fury so succinct, that the edge of her blade was dull by comparison.

She'd used that violent fervor to hone her body and her mind and her magic—all for this day.

Yet, as her parents stood across from her, their expressions as uncaring as the winter night—she found herself struggling to maintain that element of normalcy. The slight fidgets and minor quirks were what made people at ease. Made them comfortable. She'd learned in this very house how to manipulate reactions with her body, even when her mind would never, and could never, work the same as theirs.

"What do you want, Quinn?" Percinius asked, seeing through the thinly veiled attempt that her dark emotions were making it hard to keep contained.

"A decent family, a thicker cloak, maybe hot dinner and a man to please me." She tapped her chin and said, "But alas, I'm only going to get three of those."

Her father's jaw tensed, his lips pushing together.

"I will not ask again," he dared to threaten.

"Alright," she replied, equal amount of ice entering her tone. She came around the front of the lounge to stand not five feet from the people that birthed her, that raised her, and ultimately, cast her aside for something she couldn't control. No, that wasn't quite right, but it was close enough. "Where's my sister?" she asked.

Without pausing to think, her father replied, "Loralye has been married, and now has a house of her own."

"Well, then, if she's already married, let's pray that the gods are either kind or intelligent—either will do—and she never begets a child of her own to treat as poorly as you two have," Quinn replied. Percinius' eyes flashed, but it was Ethel that spoke.

"How *dare* you—"

"Tell it as it is?" Quinn said. She strode forward, the tips of her boots only inches from their sloped wooden shoes. Her chin tilted up and she turned from her father, who wasn't much larger than her anymore—to her mother who she'd grown half a head taller than. "You may have the rest of them fooled into thinking that you were the loving, doting parents to two highborn daughters, but I know the truth of what you really are." She leaned forward and lifted a hand to brush down her mother's cheek.

Ethel flinched, and Quinn didn't even possess the feeling to be hurt by that.

Not anymore.

"Spare me the lesson in propriety and manners. I came for my sister. Where is she?" Black tendrils wafted off her finger, gently caressing her mother's pale cheek. Fear stirred at her touch and Ethel shuddered. Percinius spoke.

"Loralye—"

"I don't want to know about that *cunnus*," she snapped. Percinius raised his arm sharply, intending to backhand her. Quinn's free hand came up and her fingers wrapped around his wrist, nails biting into the thin, aging flesh. Her eyes flashed an iridescent blue as she let a fraction of her hatred show through as she gazed upon her father. "You sold a thirteen-year-old girl to slave traders. I wasn't strong enough to fight back then. I am now." Crimson gathered around her nails as they broke the skin. If he felt pain, Percinius didn't show it. "And I would think twice, if I were you, before raising your hand to me again, *Father*," she spat the word at his feet and dropped both hands, stepping away.

"It seems the rumors we'd heard of the slave-masters down south weren't true if they haven't managed to beat that evil out of you," he replied icily.

She smiled, but there was no joy in it.

Only cruelty.

"No more than you yourself could," she replied. "Next time you attempt to strike me, I'll remove a limb."

Ethel gasped, but that glint in Percinius' gaze only deepened. They thought her evil for the magic that chose her. Damnable, even. They were high-born after all. Quinn saw the secrets and the desires that hid in the shadows, though. She might be a dark Maji, and even a spiteful woman, but at least she admitted what she was, unabashedly.

Unlike the abusive father and cowardly, neurotic mother she had.

Oh no, they'd never admit to the evil that existed in their hearts.

Her blood was just as red, splattered on the white marble floor as it was down south, dripping from the wooden slave posts.

"Loralye is the only sister you've had and ever will have," Percinius said through gritted teeth after a heavy moment.

Quinn tilted her head. The blood congealing

around her cuticles. "You want to play pretend?" she asked. "Alright, then where is your servant girl? You know the one I mean—she looks strikingly similar in many ways to the woman that birthed her." Quinn's focus found Ethel with a concentrated intention.

They exchanged a look, and while it was short, there was no denying the singular emotion that ran through them both. She could see, feel, and smell it on their skin.

Fear.

"We don't have a servant," Ethel said eventually. Quinn narrowed her eyes, her patience growing thin. Lazarus or one of the others were bound to notice her missing soon, and she wasn't quite ready to tell them the whole of what needed to be done or what had already been done.

"Where is Risk?" she asked, her tone breaking a little on her sister's name. The only sister she would recognize in her heart.

"Mariska died."

It was all he said, but those words were the very words that sealed his fate. Those words as they fell from her father's lips were the very grave he would be buried in. Quinn's vision bled red for a brief moment and shadows began to take shape. Creatures of fear brought forth from the most depraved parts of her souls started to take shape.

Quinn clenched her fingers, biting the inside of her cheek. She tasted blood and it held her together for the moment. Her gaze grew cold, harder than even the stone from which the temples of the gods had been cut.

"Died?" She repeated the word slowly, as if tasting it upon her tongue.

Her mother slowly nodded as her father stared on, his expression detached.

"Died," he repeated. Her eyes narrowed.

"How?" Quinn asked. Noting the tremble to her mother's form. Something about this didn't seem right. Didn't line up with the parents she remembered. "If she's really dead, then tell me how she died."

They were too cowardly to kill their own children.

She knew that better than anyone.

"She killed herself several years ago," her father said. "Weighed down her pockets with stones and drowned herself in the ocean. It was a tragedy." His words were chilled, unfeeling as they were rehearsed.

"You're lying," Quinn said.

"No, he's not—" her mother started, but Percinius held up a hand, silencing his wife, and like the good sheep she was, Ethel lowered her head.

"I can assure you, the servant girl you remember is long gone. If that's what you've returned for, then you'll be sorely disappointed."

Contempt swirled inside of her as her heart slowed and her vision sharpened. Quinn curled her fingers into fists but kept herself from reaching for the knife under her tunic, or the compacted staff swinging idly at her hip.

"You're good, Father. I'll give you that, but Risk would never kill herself. She was too strong for that." Quinn took several steps toward him. "I will find her, wherever she is, and when I do—there will be nothing left standing between you and what I came for."

Percinius leaned in, his pale blue, near-white eyes glaring at her.

"You'll never find her," he whispered.

"We'll see about that."

It was the only answer she gave, and then she stepped around him and showed herself out. The door clicked softly behind her as glacial winds whipped at her cloak. She didn't bother drawing the hood in these conditions. Skadi was either raging along with her or celebrating, but either way, the makings of an ice storm were stirring in the northern lands.

Quinn took to the streets, but she didn't return back to the others. Not yet. The idea of Risk even possibly being dead . . . she shook her head. She wasn't dead. Quinn meant what she said to them. Her sister was too strong to commit suicide. Too determined to live. She wouldn't believe it any more than she would have if they'd said they had killed her themselves.

But that only brought about other questions . . . harder ones.

If she wasn't dead, where was she? Quinn grimaced to think what they'd done to Risk in her absence. She would find her before they left this godsforsaken land.

But in what state?

That was the question.

Her father was certain that she wouldn't find her, which meant she was hidden well beyond what they thought Quinn could reach. Searching up and down, house to house wouldn't do. Roaming the streets wasn't any more effective either, but a great way to get frostbite and lose a limb. No, she'd have to find another way.

"What were you doing back there?" a voice asked out of the shadows. Lazarus materialized from seemingly thin air, and Quinn narrowed her eyes, setting her hands on her hips.

"Following me? Again?" she asked.

"Answer the question," he replied. His hair had grown over these last months, and the stubble of his jaw now thick as twine. A light layer of frost coated those hairs. The scar that ran from above his left eyebrow and clean down to his cheek stood out starkly against his tanned skin. His stare bore into her, waiting for a response.

"It's customary to be with family after going away for any time, even a ten-year interlude," she said. "I needed to speak to them. My reasons have little to do with your alliance."

Lazarus frowned. "You left without saying a word and meet with your parents that you haven't seen in ten years—and you want me to simply ignore this? I ask your reasons so I can be assured that my trust wasn't ill-placed, Quinn."

She sighed, irritation lancing through her. "If you trusted me as I asked, as you say you do, you wouldn't need my reason for every little thing I do.

Yet, it seems that out of all your vassals, I'm the only one you follow and make demands of. Why is that, Lazarus? Why did you really follow me tonight?"

He stood there, silent and brooding. She quirked an eyebrow, waiting for his response. He scrubbed a hand down his face and shook it once, flicking the droplets of melted ice away from him. "N'skara was your home. You won't tell me your reasons for leaving, nor what you're doing sneaking around at night. What would you have me do, Quinn? Ignore it? I don't demand things of Draeven or Dominicus or Lorraine because they don't act as you do. They don't test my limits, nor try my patience."

Quinn grit her teeth, but didn't snap back. It wouldn't help her here. "I asked for trust while we're here. Is it really so hard for you?"

"Yes." She froze, not expecting an answer— certainly not an honest one. "It may seem a simple thing that I don't tend to my other vassals in the way that I do with you, but you forget, they've been with me for years. They've earned my trust. You've been with me for mere months, and just as you ask for it, you never give it." She didn't argue that, even if the urge to fight was raring inside her.

"I'm not ready," she said, turning away. He didn't say anything, so she continued. "I know that you want answers, but I can't give them yet. Not while things are still so . . . unresolved." *Yes, because that's the best way to refer to what you intend on the N'skari Council.* "I need time."

"We only have ten days," he said.

"Then give me the ten days and you'll have your answers," she replied hastily.

"Alright," he answered. She blinked, her head whipping up to stare at him.

"Alright?" she repeated. "That's it? None of your usual, 'you're being unreasonable and irrational'?" She imitated his voice. Lazarus cocked an eyebrow, giving her a sidelong glance.

"You asked for ten days. Would you rather I argue and make this more difficult—or wait the short period and have you talk willingly?" he responded. "I might not be the most patient man, but I recognize how to choose my battles. I'll give you your space, because what you're giving me back is worth far more than those days."

She stared a second longer before nodding, and as they walked back toward their accommodations in silence, Quinn couldn't help but notice that things were changing between them. The tension that had always been there had grown from a violent maelstrom to quiet as the night—and just like the darkness, it slithered in her veins and under her skin.

Fighting with Lazarus was explosive, but this—whatever it was—had become so much more.

Visions of Delirium

"Freedom is given to few, while hope is given to all."
— *Mariska Darkova, prisoner*

There was no light in the shadows. No minuscule stream of brightness to illuminate her tiny cell. What was worse—the entire cage reeked of death. And yet, here she was—still alive. Barely.

A rattle echoed in her chest as she wheezed, struggling for breath. While her mind had long ago given up on the offering of air and life, her body, it seemed, had yet to face the grim reality of her circumstances.

Sometimes, she felt the call of a beast deep inside of her. It urged her to fight, to live. But today, that creature was gone and all that remained was a skeleton made of regret and exhaustion.

Weary eyelids struggled to lift. The slow drip of water somewhere in the corner of her cell called to her. Beyond her line of sight, she saw her arm lift toward it, the limb a pale gray, near white, when once it had been a slate color. Fingers reached out, grasping, palm turned upward to cup just a little bit of the liquid in her hand, but wherever the water was, it was too far. Just like everything else.

Bones that had once carried her up and down narrow staircases several times a day were now too weak to stand and everything else remained out of her reach—including salvation and freedom. Her body was as breakable as glass. The feeling of resignation welled up from the depths of her soul—a sick, twisted emotion that had kept her company all these years. If it had, in fact, been years. There was no window by which she could count the days. Perhaps misery made time seem like an eternity in her mind. Then again, as she stared down at her arms and legs, she recognized that she had grown since being put in here. She had developed into a young woman, but still more closely resembled an emaciated corpse.

Risk coughed, her vision darkening—blurring until nothing of the prison around her remained in sight. It was time, she decided. As if that would allow her descent into Beliphor's embrace and convince Mazzulah to come for her. To take her off to the Dark Realm, because anything—even death—would be far preferable to living in a damp hole, used, spit on, damaged again and again. Anything . . .

Anything?

Risk's own body couldn't find the strength to show a physical start, but her vision cleared, and she attempted to twist her head toward the sound. She hadn't heard another voice in so long—only the voices that came to take from her that which had already been taken, her dignity and pride.

Twin orbs of gold stared at her from somewhere amidst the gloom. They were beautiful pools of clear honey. They made her want to reach out, to find them in the obscurity of the room.

Would anything be better than this? The same voice filtered through her ears and for a split moment, Risk darted a glance to the sole door that led in and out of what would likely be her crypt.

"Yes." The first of any word to have left her lips in a long time and it came out as a struggling whisper on the driest of tongues.

I see.

"Who—" Risk broke off her question as she tried to lick her chapped lips, the sound of her unfinished question weak.

You can speak to me this way. I will hear it, the voice said.

Risk gave up on getting her feeble voice a chance to resurface. *Who are you?*

That is up to you, they answered.

Risk frowned. *What do you mean? What is your name?*

It is whatever name my master gives me.

Risk sighed. The voice was driving her in circles. She was sure it didn't mean to do so, it was, after all, likely another phantom and had no thought of its own. Take food and drink away for too long and hunger had the opportunity to play tricks on a person's mind.

I am no trick, the voice said in a tone that suggested it was affronted by the mere suggestion.

In an attempt to shake the illusion away, Risk's cheek turned and slid against the grimy wall, streaking her skin with yet more of the dark green gunk that grew on the ice-cold stone.

Of course, you are, Risk replied. And while this one was strange, it was not so terrifying as some of her other visions of delirium. Not yet, at least.

I am not, the voice snapped. Following the outcry was the sound of feathers sliding against air.

Wings? Risk thought.

Yes. They are my wings, the voice answered her unspoken confusion.

You have wings? Risk felt her chest rise sharply. A longing stung at her insides. She had always wanted wings. Something to take her far away from this bastille. Risk couldn't help but indulge her addled mind. If she was to die, then why not indulge in the lunacy while it was pleasant. *What color are they? Where have your wings taken you?*

They are the color of night, the voice answered. *And they have taken me many places, but no place as important as here.*

Risk had not thought it possible to laugh anymore. She thought that ability had been beaten out of her by now, but a stale rasping chuckle escaped from between her lips.

This place is important? she inquired, her jaded amusement plain.

It is not so much the place, but the person that inhabits it.

Risk's smile disappeared. Her laughter drained away.

I am not a person. I am nothing. No one.

Vile.

Corrupt.

Evil.

Tainted.

Raksasa.

The reminder cut at her, biting at what she had thought were long dead emotions, riling her irritation. Her anger. When before there had been nothing but a willingness to succumb to the void.

You are but one of those things, and you are not alone, Mariska. You have never been alone. There are those who have watched you when they can do no more, and there are those who would come for you. Risk blinked. The creature had called her by name. She had not heard another being say her name or even acknowledge that she had one in . . . a long while. The creature kept talking. *You believe that you will die here, but what will you do if you don't? What will you do if you grow wings?*

A part of Risk wanted to curse the voice for its unnecessary questions. They only served to make Risk think of things she had long ago lost hope for.

Yet, there was a kernel of that hope that still existed, small though it was. Risk knew her answer.

Moving slowly, she raised her head from where it slumped to the side and let it fall with a thump against the stone at her back. Her vision wavered, but in the shadows before her the shape of a bird—large, elegant, and still with those glowing spheres the same color as the sun—stared back. The animal was large, impossibly so. She could dimly make out the lines of the bars behind it—the reminder of her cage and the men who guarded it beyond, somewhere else in the darkness.

I would fly away, she said. Even her internal voice was kept low, a whisper so that no one else might hear what she kept deep within her heart. *I'd fly far away, and I'd never return. I would grow strong, stronger than anyone ever believed I could be—*

Even yourself? the bird asked.

Yes, she said immediately. *I'd be far stronger than I've ever been before. Strong enough to defend myself from anyone who would hurt me again.* In her mind, she would be enough to take her revenge on those who already had.

Good, it answered, those shimmering orbs of daylight bobbing. *Then perhaps you should not give into the temptation of oblivion so readily. Perhaps if you were to hold on a bit longer, you would realize that you are soon to take flight.*

Risk longed for that. More than water or food. More than sleep without nightmares. More than anything else in the world. The familiar feeling of hope wasn't new. It was as though the creature had laid another piece of wood upon the hearth of her flagging life to remind her.

Only one other person had ever been able to do that.

Quinn.

Quinn wasn't here, though. She couldn't be. Quinn had been sold. She was leagues away from this temple of depravity.

Risk stared openly at the bird, examining its shape, the stillness of its body. *Was it too much to wonder who had sent this creature to her? And why now?* she thought.

I have always been with you, Mariska, the creature said—its voice and presence somehow deep within her mind.

My . . . friends call me Risk, she replied. The statement was, in part, untrue. She had never had friends before, had never been allowed. Only Quinn had ever called her Risk.

Then I will as well . . . Risk. It must have been her

imagination, but she swore that the creature had tilted its head down in a sure sign of respect, a small bow.

I want to give you a name, Risk said.

The ruffle of feathers greeted her request and then silence. For a moment, Risk worried she had scared the creature away. And then it spoke. *Do you wish to become my master?*

No. Risk desired nothing less than to be master to anyone. *I simply wish to give you a name. Will you allow me to?*

More silence, before a curious, *what would you call me if you were my master?*

Risk thought on it. What would she call a creature with wings of night and eyes of Leviticus' light?

White lips, parched of color, parted and Risk's raspy voice echoed throughout the room. "Alpis," she whispered.

What does it mean? the creature asked.

Risk relaxed her body against the stone, feeling drained. So much conversation—even if the creature was a phantom—had worn her down. Oblivion encroached. Another endless sleep filled with nightmares she'd held at bay and she could no longer refuse its presence.

Risk? The flap of wings. *What does the name mean?*

With the last of her mental strength, just before her mind winked out like a star disappearing from the night sky, she answered with the same thing that might see her to what she truly desired—her freedom.

It means . . . her chest rattled as she breathed and fought back the wave of unconsciousness that leeched at her.

Risk? The voice of the creature sounded far away, echoing in her head.

Hope, she finally managed to answer. *The name means Hope.*

Crumbling Pedestals

"A comfortable man is a blind man, and a blind man is easy to kill."
— *Quinn Darkova, vassal of House Fierté, fear twister, white raksasa, second daughter of the Darkova Household*

The more things changed, the more they stayed the same. At least that was what Quinn was beginning to realize as she and Lazarus strode through the streets several days later while waiting for his audience to begin. She'd left N'skara as a slave and returned a free woman, freer than she'd ever been before the bonds of slavery. She was a different person now. Older. Wiser. Changed both inside and out—but the N'skari had not. Lower born still wore the gray robes of submission. Higher born and Maji still cowed those they deemed beneath them. While all were 'equal,' some were more equal than others.

No, N'skara hadn't changed in any noticeable way.

But there were subtle differences—makings of a slow but steady cultural shift that reflected that of the world they so tried to isolate themselves from.

As they made their way through the ice-land city of Liph, Quinn noticed on more than one occasion, the low born struggling with the physical labor required of them. One man in particular carried two hefting sacks of rice, imported from some land south of here. His frame was sturdy but aging, and his knees wobbled as he tried to make the ascent from the docks to the inner-city store-house where all goods were transported for inspection before being distributed to the general public. Quinn saw it a moment before it actually happened, the way one man in a white robe strode by the other. It was nothing more than a flick of his wrist and a wayward wind too strong to be anything other than magic came barreling down the street at just the right angle to send the struggling man reeling. He didn't topple into the streets. Instead, he fell onto his other side and one bag of rice clocked the higher born in the head so hard his neck whipped around. A scuffle ensued, followed by the profuse apologies of the rice man, no mind paid to the fact that the wind whispering prick caused him to fall to begin with. However, the apologies held a tune of insincerity, of exhaustion, of defiance.

She paused and Lazarus followed suit, gazing up at the temple from the courtyard below, but still listening in on the conversation between the lower and highborn men across the way.

"How do you expect to provide me with compensation, you scortum?"

"I do apologize, sir, as I've said, I cannot—"

"Cannot or will not?" the highborn interrupted with a huff.

There was a brief pause and Quinn wished for all the world to turn around and see the expression on the lower born man's face. She would have bet everything she had, from her position as Lazarus' vassal to the clothes off her back, that it did not portray the sufficient amount of respect, subservience, and reticence that the highborn expected and believed he was due, despite being the cause of it.

In the next instance, she was proven right. "You're not sorry at all."

A few more insults and curses were thrown out before the white-robed bigot kept moving. Quinn glanced over her shoulder as the rice man rolled his eyes. He noticed Quinn, standing on the edge of the street, her curious stare on him. Quinn's lips twitched ever so slightly as the man froze, fear of reprisal rising in his expression until she shook her head and turned away as a small smile spread across her lips.

It seemed that while little had changed, something in the common people had.

"When will we go in?" Lazarus asked, drawing her attention away from the man.

"When they call for us," Quinn replied.

"And when will—"

Lazarus was interrupted by the approach of a servant of one of the Council families, a pin upon his chest naming the Sorvent House he was connected with. "Quinn Darkova, second daughter of the Darkova Household?" Quinn tilted her chin at the call of her name and the man—a boy, really —in traditional gray robes blinked and ducked his head slightly as he spoke. "The Council has gathered and awaits your presence in the temple."

"It's time," she translated to Lazarus.

Quinn nodded to the messenger and started past the man—who quickly scrambled to get out of her way—Lazarus followed behind and they climbed the stairs to the temple in resolute silence. As they entered the main chancel, Quinn frowned, scanning the pedestals, two of which were empty. It didn't escape her notice that one of the councillors missing was Edward and so, too, were her parents —the heads of House Darkova.

Quinn leveled Elder Emsworth with a look as the doors behind her and Lazarus were shut— closing out the sounds filtering in from the streets of Liph. "We were told that the Council had been gathered," she stated.

Elder Emsworth's wrinkled face didn't even twitch at the disrespect clear in her tone. He merely waved an age spot-speckled hand at the empty seats and said, "Unfortunately, not all councillors are willing to hear your foreign friend speak."

Unfortunate, it was. Quinn clenched her teeth for a moment, but to be honest, four of the council- lors and the Elder were already a much better turnout than she had originally expected. Twisting back to Lazarus, Quinn relayed this information.

He nodded; his expression unreadable. "Tell

them that I thank them for coming here, then, to listen to me."

Quinn didn't much like being in this position —as both translator and mediator—but it was what she had agreed to and it was a small price to pay for what Lazarus was truly giving her. Pivoting to face Elder Emsworth once more, Quinn spoke.

"Lord Fierté thanks you for coming, and he wishes you to know that you are wise to allow him this audience, for he has much to propose."

"No guarantees will be made, Quinn," Elder Emsworth replied. "We agreed on an audience, nothing more. It would not do to get the man's hopes up."

Leveling the elder with a hard stare. Quinn spoke again, this time, the meaning solely hers. "Regardless of the lack of guarantee," she said, "it would behoove you and all of N'skara to give credence to this man's plans for the future. You cannot outlast the change of this world with how you currently rule."

Someone sucked in their breath and Quinn's gaze flickered to the woman in question who sat forward, a long, thick white braid hanging over one shoulder. "How *dare* you," she hissed. "What could you possibly know? You've not been here for nigh ten years. You insinuate—"

"I insinuate nothing," Quinn interrupted the woman. "I state it outright."

The scene in the street hadn't left her thoughts, remaining behind to plague her mind. There was a hint of something there—that defiance that sparked a recognition in her.

"What exactly are you stating then?" Amenival of House Bireni—a man of great age, but not so great as the elder—inquired.

Quinn faced the man in question. "I'm merely stating that you should listen to what Lazarus has to say, preferably before you decide to ignore his words."

The man lifted his bearded face and fixed a scowl on another councillor. "This girl has grown far too outspoken. She is sacrilegious." He punctuated his outcry with a hard fist against his pillar, making the whole thing shudder.

Quinn stared, stone-faced, as the elder sighed and with great restraint, cast her a hard look even as the other councillor went on, making his dislike and distrust of her quite clear.

Lazarus stepped up to Quinn's side and

narrowed his eyes at her. "What did you say?" he demanded.

Quinn shrugged and answered, "I merely pointed out that it would benefit them to listen to your proposal."

Before Lazarus could respond, the elder brought his hand down upon his own stool repeatedly, calling the attention of the angered councillor. "Enough," he called in his deep, raspy voice. "Speak your piece, Quinn Darkova and Lord Fierté. We have work to do."

Quinn nodded to Lazarus that it was time. Taking a deep breath, he stepped forward and began to speak. Quinn regarded him, the way his arms moved, his focus moving from one councillor to the next until they landed squarely on the elder and then remained there, direct and confident. Quinn translated as quickly as she was able, keeping her focus on the expressions of the councillors. Even as he spoke, they kept their faces either impassive, downright bored, or condescending. The woman from before kept her lips pursed, her eyebrow lifted. Amenival merely blinked in impassioned boredom. Finally, the drone of words seemed to be too much for him, and he cut Quinn's next translation off with a sharp bark.

"What do we get out of it?" Amenival demanded.

"What do you get out of it?" Quinn repeated as Lazarus faced the man.

Lazarus sent Quinn a seeking look and she quickly translated before leveling the man, Amenival, with a glare. "It would benefit both of our countries if the N'skari were to form an alliance," Lazarus said calmly, a repeat of an earlier point. He continued, but as Quinn saw the man—Amenival —narrow his attention on Lazarus with contempt, she translated and repeated Lazarus' words back to him. "As I've previously explained, I now have ties with the Ciseans and the Ilvans—"

"Why would you need ties with the N'skari, then?" Amenival interrupted. "You are Norcastan. Far to the south. We are the north. You have nothing we could want and yet, you try to win us over with your flowery words and tell us how important it is that we join your alliance. We have been independent for hundreds of years and have proven how capable we are as a people. This audience is nothing more than a farce."

"If this audience is nothing more than a farce, then you are nothing more than a fool," Quinn said sharply, her words cutting like a dagger to the man's throat. Lazarus jerked his face toward her, uncomprehending of the words that spilled from her mouth, but clearly aware of the tone of her voice. She turned her attention to the rest of the room. Though they'd been listening, finally giving at least some modicum of consideration to Lazarus and his alliance, it was obvious that they were still unsure, and it was time to change that, to reveal to them the reality of their situation.

"The world as you know it is changing," Quinn stated. "There is a shift, but the N'skari are too blind to see it. All you see here is what you want to see—an antiquated image of the past. N'skara is cut off from most of the world, protected by the ice and frost you create. But a downfall *is* possible. If you agree to align yourselves with the future king of Norcasta, you gain an ally in the world you know nothing about—the world that could destroy you. More than that, you gain connections to not only Norcasta, but to Ilvas and the Ciseans as well."

"Bah," the woman from before scoffed. "An alliance with pirates and barbarians. How preposterous."

"Better preposterous than dead," Quinn pointed out solemnly.

"An alliance with N'skara has never happened

before," Elder Emsworth said, the low rumble of his voice drawing everyone's attention.

Quinn nodded to him. "And if you don't change, it never will."

"What makes you believe we need an alliance to keep our way of life, Quinn?" Elder Emsworth asked. Before she could reply, he continued. "As Norlinda has stated before, we are a proud and capable people. An alliance would be like asking for assistance when we do not need it."

"An alliance is not asking for anything," Quinn corrected him. "An alliance is a promise—to be there in times of strife should you need it."

Elder Emsworth released another sigh, one clearly meant as a statement. He was not interested —none of them were. They didn't care about the world outside of their frost-coated corner. They thought themselves above the rest, demigods among humans. The closest mankind could come to the realm of the sacred without actually existing within it.

"I believe this meeting has come to a close. Your request for an alliance is denied," Elder Emsworth said with cool detachment. "I hope you'll consider staying with us, Quinn, when your friends' time in N'skara comes to an end."

Quinn felt her own anger rise, a sharp spike up her spine accompanied by dark whispers in her ear. Little prods that told her she could destroy them all and show them how very vulnerable they actually were. Lazarus' hand on her arm was the only thing that stopped her and brought her crashing back down to reality.

"They are not ready," he said.

Quinn blinked at him, confused at first, then surprised. He couldn't understand a lick of what had been said, but Lazarus was no fool. He had read the room. The faces of the councillors were closed off, uninterested, and downright hostile.

With a slow inhale, Quinn lifted her head and her gaze met that of the elder. "This is not over," she said coldly.

Norlinda's lip curled in condescension, and her expression was mirrored upon the others' faces. Elder Emsworth shook his head. "We agreed, Quinn. You received your audience. A deal is a deal."

"Amenival was right," she announced. "This audience *was* a farce. Until you agree to give Lazarus Fierté a true audience—one in which you actually listen"—Quinn cut her eyes across the room, fixating on each councillor for just long enough that they began to shift uncomfortably —"that is when your promise of an audience will be fulfilled. This was nothing more than a waste of time."

With that, Quinn spun, grabbing Lazarus by the arm and steering him before her. Lazarus' lips curled down and he removed his limb from her grip immediately, but he didn't deny her the exit. Together, they left the temple and stepped back out onto the streets of Liph. Quinn sought the area where the lower born rice man had been, but he was long gone.

"That didn't go well," Lazarus commented.

Quinn shook her head. "No, it didn't, but it could've gone worse." Much worse. She knew.

Lazarus glanced at her. "Oh?"

Her lips twitched as she descended the temple's steps and he followed. "Neither of us were beheaded or dismembered."

Lazarus' expression was part shock and part something Quinn couldn't read. She turned to him as he came alongside her. "They do not imprison people, then?" he asked.

"No," Quinn replied. "They simply kill them."

It was the N'skari way—to kill or get rid of anything that you didn't like or that didn't agree with you. It was what her parents had done with her, after all, and what she was sure they did with Risk. She had to find out where they put her—she knew Risk wasn't dead and they certainly wouldn't have blamed the loss of two children to slave traders. Not even the N'skari would overlook that.

Quinn cracked her neck as she and Lazarus strode down the street, heading back the way they'd come. One way or another, she would find the answers she sought.

An Invitation in Propriety

"The customs of the past bind us in ways only we allow."
— Quinn Darkova, vassal of House Fierté, fear twister,
white raksasa, second daughter of the Darkova Household

Two knocks sounded from the front door.

Quinn paused, glancing over her hand of cards to the four sitting around her.

"I'm not gettin' it," Axe proclaimed, leaning back in her chair and swinging her legs up one by one to rest her boots on the edge of the table.

"Vaughn," Quinn said, hooking a thumb toward the girl.

The mountain man peered over and said,

"Little pirate should not put feet on table. She-wolf Quinn does not approve." Axe responded by blowing a piece of her crimson hair from her face and eyeing him. Once she established that neither of them were joking, she groaned. Her boots dropped away from the table, leaving behind mud stains.

Draeven started chuckling, folding his cards facedown on the table. "The day I see a barbarian give a pirate lessons on table manners," he paused, shaking his head. "We're not in Norcasta anymore."

"No," Dominicus said, glancing up from his cards to the rest of them and frowning. "We're certainly not." He drew from the pile and tossed down a spare, before laying his hand out for them to see. "That's Rikkers," he said, the faintest hints of a smile gracing his usually stony exterior.

"Black Baac!" Axe yelled, leaning forward to examine the cards. She narrowed her eyes when she saw no fault. Both Vaughn and Draeven sighed. Quinn shook her head, getting to her feet to answer the door as another set of knocks came.

She grasped the chilled metal in one hand and pulled, unsure what to expect, but a servant in gray robes with the emblem of House Arvis on it wasn't it.

"Yes?" Quinn asked the young girl. No more than Axe's age, it struck her for a moment, the vast difference between the outlandish child gambling away half her inheritance at the table, and the creature before her. Silver-haired and pale skinned, she appeared much the same as the other N'skari. Her tiny, frail form stood unmoving despite the cold chill that had descended on them. She glanced up with pale blue eyes. Whereas Axe's glowed with happiness and amusement more often than not, this child held only emptiness in her expression.

Quinn frowned when the girl extended two hands from her robe. Clasped between them was a silver tray, and on it a piece of fine parchment, folded neatly.

She took it and cracked the dark blue wax seal that held it closed.

Inside, in elegant script, the message she'd both anticipated and dreaded, awaited.

An invitation. One that, much as she wanted to, could not be turned down.

"What is it?" Draeven asked, coming up beside her. In the background, she could hear Axe spitting curses and Vaughn attempting to calm the 'little pirate'.

"We have dinner plans," she murmured. The

parchment felt stiff between her numbing fingers. Seeing her parents was one thing, and as awful as that was, she dreaded this more.

"We do?" Draeven asked. "With who?"

She sighed heavily and thanked the child. The girl was already out of view when Quinn finally closed the door and answered. "Tell Lazarus and the others to be ready before nightfall." She pivoted, peering over nothing in particular as images from the past surfaced and the skilled hands of a water weaver threatened to pull her under. She shook the vision off and felt Neiss moving beneath her flesh, silently aiding her as she said, "My sister's expecting us."

Quinn left the main room to retreat to the bedroom she'd been placed in. Inside, the furniture was sparse. A single bed made of ashwood, a night-stand, and a dresser. Overall, the room was as unfeeling and impersonal as her welcome home had been. She looked out the moderately sized window into the gray beyond. Thick heavy clouds were on the horizon. With temperatures dropping and the winter solstice upon them, that storm was bound to be an icy one.

The more she looked out at the barren land-scape beyond, the seashell and mortar streets, the eggshell plaster homes, the snow flurries drifting in from over the ocean . . . the more she found herself thinking back. This time, not of that night itself, but the incident that caused it.

It was the day she learned the truth.

And she paid for it.

Her fingers toyed with the stiff cloth of the drapes as the memories pulled her under.

THE VIEW OF LIPH BEFORE HER WAS REPLACED BY that of an empty fountain she knew of that resided in the lower born ghettos of the city. Once it would have ran with clean water, but ever since the magic that kept N'skara frozen came into play, water no longer ran. A statue of the deity Mazzulah stood. Its face and body a mismatched mix of white and gray stone, making it grotesque in a way.

Quinn said as much, frowning in dislike at the missing marble facing, that gave way to an uglier inside.

"I think it's beautiful," Risk had said. She was young then. Her gray skin a shade lighter than the stone. Her hair was silver, like all the N'skari, and worn long. She'd never be one of them though. On her head, two tiny black horns jutted out, no further than an inch.

"It's missing pieces," Quinn said, motioning with one hand. Risk shrugged; her gray robes too loose for her petite form.

"It's old. Anything that old loses pieces along the way. People do too." She walked over to the side, and picked up a chunk of marble, holding it up to the sun. "Sometimes you find them again, though, and you cherish it more." The girl walked over, her bare feet dirty as she climbed on top of the fountain's edge and walked across its frozen surface. She stood before it and put the tiny chunk of marble back exactly where it belonged on the statue's face. The god smiled. So was Risk, when she turned around.

Quinn sighed, a smile of her own beginning to blossom when she heard a voice.

"What are you doing here?"

Quinn twisted around, already grimacing from her elder sister's high-pitched tone. "We're looking at the fountain. Obviously."

Loralye pressed her perfect lips together. "Don't you have lessons with Sister Rowe this morning?"

"Finished," Quinn shrugged. It wasn't a complete truth, but close enough. Today had been singing, and for all her skill in dance, she lacked that and more in her voice. The good sister had lost patience and excused her from her lessons, claiming she needed to see a practitioner about her hearing.

"Then you should be in temple," Loralye said.

"And you should mind your own business," Quinn replied back. "But here we all are."

She could see it then and she remembered it crystal clear, the way Loralye's expression tightened. She smiled, but it was all teeth.

"You shouldn't speak to your betters that way," her sister said.

Quinn looked around, very exaggerated, before facing Loralye once more. "Perhaps, but I don't see one around." Behind her, Risk snorted. A stone settled in her stomach as her sister looked up at the servant girl.

"You're going to pay for that comment," she snapped.

Her hand extended outward. The blood in Quinn's veins bubbled. *Literally.*

"Lora, you shouldn't do—" Risk started. Quinn closed her eyes.

Stupid girl. She should never have done that. For like their parents, the thing her sister cared about the most, was her image.

"Don't you tell me what I should or should not do, you raksasa," Loralye snapped. Her fingers curled and the blood in Quinn's body pushed and pulled and downright stopped. Every unnatural tug sent her into a fit of pain so great the edges of her vision darkened. She felt herself beginning to black out, and she welcomed it.

The darkness meant the pain was over, at least for a time.

This time she was not so lucky.

"No!" Risk shouted. Quinn heard the cawing of a bird. Her eyes snapped open as not a single bird, but a flock of hundreds attacked Lorlaye.

Her sister screamed for a moment, and then one by one the birds began to drop to the ground. They had no corpses. Only pieces of them.

Quinn knew it because she'd seen the bird her sister exploded for fun. When one of the sisters, or heaven forbid their parents caught her, she'd claim it was a sacrifice in thanks to the gods for her gifts. But she knew the truth.

Bird after bird began to drop and the squawking quickly turned to alarmed cries. "No, no," Risk cried. Quinn turned to see their servant and her friend, with tears streaming down her face. "She's killing them," Risk sobbed.

"Shhh," Quinn whispered, embracing her quickly. She leaned down so that they were eye level and said, "Stop them or she'll kill them all."

"But if I stop them, she'll go after you—" Risk protested.

"Send them away. I can handle my sister."

Risk swallowed, looking between the fallen birds and the ones still attacking, to Quinn whose skin likely looked like she had the pocks. Whenever Loralye used her water weaving powers on her, the vessels near the surface of her skin always burst first, leaving her ugly. Her mother would act as if it were the sun and tell her to stay inside more. That being among others wasn't safe, but being in that house wasn't safe either. So, Quinn did what she always did, and eventually Loralye always caught up.

The birds scattered the moment Risk released them from her power and standing there amongst blood and body parts was Loralye. Her white robes were torn, and claw marks nicked her skin. Her lovely face was now as ugly as Quinn's surely was. The glower on it didn't help.

"You!" she spat, pointing at Risk. She quaked where she stood. "How dare you attack me—"

"How dare you attack me?" Quinn snapped. "She was protecting me, and you know it."

Loralye lifted a hand to her face and when her fingers came away red, she blanched. Over the span of seconds, though it felt like forever, it was such a short fuse that lit and went off. Quinn felt her power gathering in the air. Dark tendrils wafted up from Quinn's skin as her sister pointed a finger at them both and said a single word.

"Bleed."

She had been tortured before. She'd been beaten, slapped, kicked, and bled—many, many times.

None of them were like this, though. This all-consuming pain as her skin split open and her life began to run. Rivers of red. She'd remember it, she thought back then, and she wasn't wrong.

All her life she'd tried to dance the careful line of who and what she should be. Her parents hated her for her magic. Her sister hated her for everything else. The only friend she'd ever had was Risk, and she was likely going to die for standing up to Loralye.

A dark thought took shape.

An even darker urge took hold. Quinn opened her eyes and lifted her head, no matter how hard it seemed. She pushed herself past the pain to sit up, despite being lowered to her knees.

Then she smiled and welcomed the fear.

For thirteen years she hid in the light. She pretended that she could be better. Do better.

All it took was mere seconds for the dark to welcome her home.

She lashed out at her sister with everything she had. Black magic poured from her skin, and was still pouring when Loralye started to scream. The sounds that came from her were like a wounded animal, but Quinn was past caring as she attacked.

She didn't understand how it worked yet. Not truly. She knew her magic came easier to her than any other she knew, but she didn't get why.

Not until she began to see images in her mind. Images of their mother giving birth. Images of a babe with gray skin, swaddled in black cloth. Flashes of memories fractured apart without reason. They all centered around one thing.

Risk.

Her servant.

Her friend.

Her . . . sister?

Quinn got to her feet, disoriented and shaking. She couldn't control the anger that was starting to overwhelm her. She'd always been a bitter child. She liked to play games. She enjoyed pushing and pushing until people snapped, because even though the results weren't kind, she learned that way. She learned about boundaries and limits and human behavior. She learned to think and act so that she could pretend she was like them.

But inside she was black.

She was fear.

"Is Risk our sister?" she asked, stumbling forward. Loralye didn't answer.

"Is Risk our sister?" she repeated. Again, she received no answer.

Deep down she knew though. It was answer enough.

She glanced over her shoulder to the unconscious girl in gray.

It was easy to see when she was looking for it. The slope of her nose. The cut of her jaw. The bow of her lips. She looked remarkably similar, because they were sisters.

And all their lives, her family had treated her as a slave.

A servant.

A raksasa.

Quinn turned back to Loralye, and something

inside her broke away. Like a piece of the statue, it fell off and what remained was ugly but true. It was the Quinn she always had been.

The Quinn she would be.

"If you won't speak with your lips, there are other ways," she whispered, kneeling in front of Loralye.

She dove into her mind. Into her memories. Quinn spliced them apart and she learned the truth.

It was terrible to behold.

A Lesson in Tradition

"The question is not what is right or wrong, for that differs based on perspective. The question is simply what is, and what is not."
— *Quinn Darkova, vassal of House Fierté, fear twister, white raksasa*

A quiet rap on her door pulled at Quinn's attention.

"Come in," she said without turning. The knob jiggled and the hinges creaked as the wooden pane swung open. Light footfalls behind her narrowed down the list of suspects. When Lorraine walked past her, approaching the corner of the bed and sitting, Quinn finally turned.

"I hear we're going to your sister's for dinner," the older woman started, picking at the wrinkles in the skirt she wore. Quinn hiked an eyebrow.

"We are," she said.

"I didn't know you had a sister," Lorraine continued.

Quinn narrowed her eyes. "If you're here to pry for Lazarus, I already told him—"

"I'd like your help getting ready, actually," the other woman responded.

Quinn froze mid-sentence, dumbfounded for a moment, but then said, "Oh. I thought—"

"—I was here for Lazarus. Yes, I know." Lorraine wrinkled her nose at that. "If Lazarus needs a spy, he asks Dominicus, if he needs a diplomat, he asks Draeven, and if he wants dinner to be edible—he asks me. I'm not here for him." Quinn took a step away from the window and examined Lorraine. In this light, the silver of her roots was more muted, a mere white against chocolate brown. She'd lost weight over the last few weeks—a result of her wound and illness. The loss showed in her figure. The way the shirt she currently wore hung loosely, the outline of her shape disappearing beneath it. But her skin was clean and not clammy, and eyes bright, if a bit tired.

"Alright." Quinn nodded. "How can I help you?"

"I'd like to make a good first impression," Lorraine stated, regarding her directly. Quinn snorted. "What?" she asked.

"How Loralye views you is unimportant. She's a cunnus," Quinn said.

"What does that mean?" Lorraine asked. Quinn tilted her head and looked at the ceiling as she weighed how to explain it.

"A dishonorable woman. Norcasta doesn't have a good equivalent, but it's an insult."

Lorraine's lips pinched together a little as she raised both eyebrows at Quinn. "I assumed as much given it was you who was saying it."

At that, Quinn cracked a smile and then let out a snort. Lorraine smirked, laughing softly under her breath. "I'd like to make a good impression regardless of what Loralye is. I am Lazarus' stewardess, and I think learning about the N'skari way would behoove me."

Quinn shook her head, all the while biting her tongue from saying *Miss Manners*, even if she did think it. "I'll help you as best I can, but don't take this as a reason to try to teach me more *manners*. I'm fine with being uncivilized."

There was a twinkle in Lorraine's eye as she nodded.

The next several minutes were spent with Quinn going up and down the stairs as she fetched bath water. Outside, the faucet to do so was cold to the touch, but the water that came out steamed in her face, and the dew left behind turned to frost within seconds. While boiling hot when she put it in the buckets, it chilled to a tepid warmth by the time she got it up the stairs and dumped into the heavy tub. Lorraine sat on the bed as Quinn set the buckets aside and began to strip out of her clothing.

Naked and bare to the world, she stepped in the tub and settled in, snatching the tiny bar of soap off the edge of the vanity where she'd left it.

"We will ready for dinner and do our hair in the traditional N'skari manner," Quinn started. She lifted a calf and scrubbed up and down with the bar of soap, massaging out the sore muscle while she did so. "When we get there, there will be no embracing. Her and I will exchange words and we'll go inside."

"Is that tradition to not embrace?" Lorraine asked. "Or is that just you?"

Her lips curled upward in a dark grin. "Both." Lorraine nodded and she continued. "Once we're inside, the table will already be set. When we sit, there is no eating nor drinking until they do so. That's important." Quinn paused to dunk her head under and when she came back up, she started to scrub at the stiff strands of hair with soap, making them slippery. "They will likely try to test this to see what I've told you, but to take anything before they do is a grave offense. If they drink, you can too. If they eat, then you may, but only after."

"Do you need help with your hair?" Lorraine asked, starting to rise from the bed.

"I've got it," Quinn answered, dunking under once more. When she came back up, she went at the mop of lavender on her head a second time. The strands loosened and the knots began to break apart.

"Very well," Lorraine said. She settled back and they sat in comfortable silence for a few moments while Quinn finished up. "I can't help but notice the color of the robes people wear here. Do they mean something?"

Quinn stood from her bath and let the water run from her in rivulets before wringing her hair with both hands. "The gray robes represent lower born and those ungifted."

"Ungifted?" Lorraine asked.

"With magic," Quinn said, stepping from the tub. "The N'skari hold Maji in the highest regard. It's the only way those of the gray can find any power in N'skari society. Though they will only become highborn if they marry one who is highborn."

Just as Quinn's mother had, not that she mentioned it to Lorraine.

The other woman appeared deeply disturbed by everything Quinn told her, though she didn't say it. Instead she asked, "Where do nulls fall into all this?"

Quinn reached for a towel and began drying herself slowly. "The N'skari condemn them. If a child is born as a null, it's cast into the ocean as a sacrifice to the goddess Myori."

Lorraine blanched. "Why?" she breathed.

"The Council is built of those in power. Those with magic. A null would be a threat to that, because magic does not affect them. Their mere existence presents a problem in the eyes of the N'skari—so it's snuffed out." Quinn reached for undergarments to begin dressing. Lorraine guarded her horror well, but she still saw it. "They won't hurt you."

"What?" Lorraine asked, her brows drawing together.

"You're a null, are you not?" she asked.

"I am." Lorraine twisted a lock of her chocolate hair, a slight frown gracing her lips. "How'd you know?"

Quinn shrugged. "I can't feel you in my field of vision," she started as she reached for her leather pants. "Lazarus left me with you the most, though he didn't trust me with seasoned soldiers." She tugged the pants on, shifting side to side as she inched them up her chilled skin. "Even if I didn't notice those things, though, your questioning is peculiar and you look scared—though I can't feel it."

Lorraine nodded, lowering her gaze as Quinn pushed her hair from her shoulders and her breasts were bare before her. She grabbed the leather top, lined with fur. It was scandalous here and not the warmest, but Quinn always did like riling Loralye up.

"I wasn't sure if it was because you tried to use your magic on me at some point . . ." Lorraine let her voice trail off. Quinn snorted.

"No," she said, moving to stand beside the other woman now that she was fully dressed. "Much as I enjoy using people's fear to get what I want, I've never tried it on you or Dominicus, or even Draeven for that matter."

Lorraine didn't comment on what she didn't say, but Quinn had a feeling she noticed the name she left off that list.

She didn't say she never used it on House Fierté, because the truth was at times, when she was feeling dangerous, reckless, unhinged—she used it on Lazarus.

Not to hurt him.

But to see what he'd do.

No, Lorraine didn't comment on that, but instead steered the conversation in a different direction. "Is what you're wearing considered appropriate for this dinner?" she asked as Quinn climbed on the bed and moved to sit behind her.

"Absolutely not," she answered. Not even Lorraine could contain her chuckle of amusement as Quinn began to part her hair.

Dinner Party

"It's easy to hate the things you don't understand, but it's even easier to hate the things you do."
— Quinn Darkova, vassal of House Fierté, fear twister, white raksasa

Several hours later, after plaiting Lorraine's hair —as well as her own—Quinn descended the stairs while securing the gold ties that kept her cloak over her shoulders. Axe glanced up at her and sucked the air between her teeth.

"You don't seem so priggish now," she said, nodding approvingly. Quinn rolled her eyes and strode past the young girl who'd been washed clean from the dirt that seemed to cling to her, never mind that all of it was buried under several feet of snow as far as the N'skari border reached.

Quinn waited for her friends and comrades as they slowly trickled over one by one.

"We're going to my sister's house. I'm not sure how much or how little Norcastan her or her husband speak, let alone their servants, so watch your words." She fired that last bit at Axe, who was busy rubbing her nose. She sniffed once, only then seeming to notice the many stares on her.

"What?" she asked, peering down at herself.

"I mean it. If it weren't for blasted tradition, I wouldn't even be bringing you lot with." She waved her hand toward Axe, Draeven, and Vaughn.

She looked at them and then shook her head, thinking it best not to ponder on it too much. If one of them was going to incur the wrath of the N'skari, they would do it with or without her warning.

Ignoring Lazarus' dark gaze that followed her every move, Quinn wrenched the door open and took to the streets. Leviticus' eye was just beginning to descend toward the horizon and with it, the slight warmth it provided. By the time they reached the road, their invitation had listed, the last of the sun had fallen right over the edge of the world and the sky was painted in shades of crimson and violet. It would only last for several minutes before the night would come and with it—the true cold.

Quinn hustled on by, not waiting for the others, but knowing they trailed behind her as she climbed to the top of the hill and found the mansion that awaited.

House Arvis. Her sister's married name now, as the letter had stated.

Quinn shook her head in mild disgust at the silver plates emblemized with the house symbol that had been mounted on the gates. The front door was made of heavy oak, chiseled into an ornately pointless design and the cracks sealed with liquid gold. The pure affluence of it compared to that of the lowborn bothered her, but not near as much as the woman that stood on the front porch.

Clad in a gown crafted from thread that gleamed as bright as starlight, Loralye stood like an ethereal goddess. Her hair hung long over her shoulder and past her waist, stopping at the tops of her thighs. She'd plaited it the same as Quinn, but instead of the red and gold ties that Quinn had used on her own hair, Loralye's were dark blue— the color of House Arvis. Powder like what she used to wear on the stage as Mirior covered her face, making her almost ghostly were it not for the painted red on her lips.

Quinn grimaced, but the cunnus she had to call sister only smiled.

On her arm stood Edward Arvis, small for a man, compared to the likes that traveled in their party, but big in ego. They were betrothed shortly before Quinn was sold into slavery, back when Loralye was considered the cream of the crop. Her water weaving abilities were truly renowned, as was her face. In Quinn's not-so-humble opinion, her personality was less so.

"Sister," Loralye said in greeting. Her voice was as brittle as ice.

Quinn nodded to them both. "My companions and I have come to pay our respects to my blood," she said in traditional greeting. Edward's watery blue eyes strayed toward the slit of her cloak to where most of her bare stomach was on display. Quinn tilted her head as his gaze slowly roamed up. He blinked when he caught her looking and then grinned like a child that knew he'd gotten away with something naughty.

"Welcome to our home," Loralye responded, equally as formal. Neither woman moved to embrace the other as she and her husband turned their backs and led the way into the open foyer. Wooden chairs, all carved as elegantly as the door and sealed with gold, sat around a set table. Porcelain plates and polished silver sat atop the whitest of napkins. In the center a wild boar had been caught and roasted with an apple in its mouth. Quinn turned to give Axe a pointed look as the girl started to cackle wildly.

"Is she mad?" Edward asked, pulling out the seat for his dear wife and then taking his own at the head.

"Sometimes," Quinn replied, taking her seat opposite of Loralye and next to Edward. Lazarus sat on her other side, and Draeven next to her sister as was tradition. While they weren't N'skari, they were Maji and that took precedence.

"So, sister, please tell me who our guests are," Loralye said, motioning to Quinn and then their group. On her left hand, the blackened ink of a wedding band was prominently tattooed and on display. Among the N'skari, marriage was an infinite contract never to be broken, no matter the reason, no matter the cost. They sealed that promise upon their flesh as vows were spoken. The very idea of being bound to a man or woman in such a way made her grimace, but she introduced her companions without hesitating. When she was done, all her sister had to say was, "hmm."

At the other end of the table, Axe started to reach for the roast pork, but Lorraine slapped her hand away before she got there. Quinn was thanking herself for explaining the proprietary rules for Lorraine now. Having someone else to watch the pirate child would make things much smoother. Loralye smiled a bit slyly, and reached out to take a drink from her cup, signifying drinking was alright. Quinn still didn't touch her cup.

"Your friends from the south are quite beastly to look at, Quinn," Edward said openly. They couldn't speak N'skaran so it wasn't like they would know, but Quinn bristled. "How do you stand to be with them and their uncivilized ways for so long?"

"Quite easily, actually," she replied, her voice about as tepid as the temperature. "You'll find that after being a slave for so many years, most anything else is manageable." Her eyes bore holes into her sister as she spoke, but the elder Darkova daughter paid it no mind, instead preferring to sip at her drink as if she'd not spoken at all.

"I'd heard you'd been sold into slavery," Edward continued. "Tell me, how was that?"

It took everything she had not to draw forth the worst of her nightmares and send them into his mind, just to see how well he held up under the tortures. Edward was a member of the Council, though, and Loralye the heir of another seat. She couldn't attack them openly without consequences.

"Horrible," Quinn answered in turn. "Imagine being trapped and chained under another's control with little to no choice in anything."

"Sometimes beasts must be contained for the greater good," Edward said. "Chained and taught its place in the world." Quinn's vision bled red as her fingers clenched into fists. Black wisps started to drift in front of her, as tantalizing as they were dangerous. "Perhaps if a god of the light has indeed brought you back, you've learned your place in the time away?"

Quinn's lips parted and she leaned forward. Eyes followed her from all around as she came inches from Edward's face and said, "If a God is indeed what led me back, you should probably pray it is not Ramiel."

"And why is that?" he asked, a sliver of fear creeping into his voice.

"Under his guidance, I would be seeking justice, and it wouldn't be merciful."

Edward had the good sense to try to suppress his shiver, but Quinn saw it, just as she saw everything else. And when she smiled at him, it was near feral.

"Now, now," Loralye started, cutting in. "We haven't even had dinner yet." She spoke softly but with a bored, disinterested tone. "Edward went out and caught the boar himself, you know."

He beamed with real pride then, drawing away from Quinn as if she would sting him, and sting him, she might still. Even so, Quinn tilted her head and said, "You can hunt? I wasn't aware that was a skill they still taught the highborn, since most are too afraid of doing any actual labor." The pride in his expression fizzled into hostile regard.

"It can be hard to find time when we're running a country and all, but I manage," he said stiffly. Quinn snorted, enjoying the way his wounded pride made his temper flare.

"Do you take days off from your busy job often? I noticed you were absent from Lord Fierté's audience this morning." His gaze narrowed and even Loralye cut her a look at that. "Or perhaps since nothing ever changes, you simply don't feel the need to do your actual job and help the people you rule over. I mean, why would you? Not when you have all this"—Quinn paused and gestured to the table spread before them before continuing—"and had to do absolutely nothing to earn it?" Edward's lips thinned, hand clenching around the fork. Her gaze flicked down to it and then back to him. She leaned in again and whispered, "Do it. I'd love to find a reason to remind you *which* daughter *I* am."

"That's enough," Loralye snapped. "Husband, you should eat. You must be famished." She served him pork while they sat in silence. Quinn and Edward glared at each other even as the others peered at them, not understanding what had transpired, only that it was best not to say anything at all.

By serving Edward pork, Loralye made it possible for the rest of them to begin eating. Quinn motioned down the table to Lorraine, who began helping Axe load roasted potatoes, seasoned turnips, and boar onto her plate. By helping, she was really ensuring that there was food left for everyone else, as Axe had the stomach of a man three times her size.

When plates were filled and people began eating, there were still two that weren't. Loralye stood from her seat and excused herself to the kitchen. Quinn pursed her lips for a moment before she, too, stood and followed after her sister, muttering an excuse simply for Edward's sake. No one else would try to stop her here.

In the corner of the Arvis Household kitchens, facing the window, Loralye stood in her dress like liquid silver, staring out into the night.

"You should be eating with the others," she said.

"How did you know I was here?" Quinn asked, knowing her footsteps made no sound on the stone floors.

"Because as you said, nothing has changed. Not even you, Sister." The elder Darkova sister took a breath before turning to face Quinn. "What do you want?"

Quinn blinked, not even surprised by the change in topic. "Why does everyone keep asking me that?" she pondered, musing aloud as she eyed the kitchen. The servants had already cleared out for the night, but she could sense them, other beings in the house with no magical talent of their own— left to serve the highborn like animals carted and ordered about.

"Because it's you," Loralye answered.

"Exactly," Quinn replied condescendingly. "It's me. You should know exactly what I want."

A pause came.

"Mariska," Loralye said eventually, her voice heavy with something—though not regret. She sighed, and Quinn tilted her head, examining her. "You won't find her," she said, all too certain and yet still, her voice quivered with a fearfulness, as if she didn't quite believe her own statement.

"Oh, I will," Quinn replied. "If you won't tell me, there are other ways, but you, above all else should know, Loralye—I always get what I want."

The other woman shuddered, the silver fabric of her dress moving with her. "And is Mariska all that you came back for?" she asked, swallowing hard. There was guilt there now, but it was too late for that. Too late for her.

"What do *you* think?" Quinn asked her.

Loralye's lips pinched together, her beautiful face turning harsh and severe as the heart in her chest. "We won't know until you do it, because that's who you are. Who you've always been. You thought we hated you for your dark powers, and while those were no blessing, it was the twisted games you played that landed you on that ship."

The corner of Quinn's mouth quirked up, because her sister was frazzled. She wasn't an idiot; she was too smart for that, and yet . . .

"I might be twisted in my games," she said.

"But the same people who made me made you, and water isn't the only thing I know you weave, big sister."

"If you so much as—" Loralye started, the blood in her veins lurching with the sudden threat. Quinn had expected it, predicted it even.

She pointed, and a tendril of darkness hit Loralye square in the chest.

Her elder sister gasped, stumbling forward. She would have fallen to her knees if Quinn hadn't stepped forward and caught her. She pressed her lips to the hollow of her ear and whispered, "Careful there, Sister, you wouldn't want to hurt yourself."

It was a warning. The only one she'd get. Her future was set in stone as far as Quinn was concerned. "You're wicked," Loralye breathed. "Evil. You don't belong here."

"I know," Quinn replied. "That's why you're going to tell dear old mom and dad that if Risk isn't on my doorstep tomorrow morning, they'll be starting a war."

Loralye swallowed, her eyes darting to the evening room beyond. "With the Norcastan Lord?"

"No," Quinn said, stepping back. "With me."

Restless Minds

"You don't have to love an honest man. You don't even have to like him. However, you do have to respect him. It takes a strong man to be honest, and that's why so few are."
— *Quinn Darkova, vassal of House Fierté, fear twister, white raksasa*

Bone-deep fatigue infiltrated her bones as she and the others marched back to their temporary accommodations. It was as though the weight of the dark realm had found her shoulders to rest upon. Lazarus had been quiet for most of the night. He hadn't even mentioned the short disappearance of her and Loralye, but she knew from his constant dark stare that he realized something was up. Quinn ignored it to the best of her ability as she climbed the staircase to her own private chambers.

She stepped inside, closing the door softly behind her. While exhausted, her mind was still mulling over too much to sleep. Thoughts of the night and the storm and all dark things plagued her.

The wind screamed down the narrow streets. The windowpane shuddered.

Quinn didn't pay it any mind as she strode across the small space and flipped the iron latch. She pressed her fingertips into the seam and slowly guided the window up, leaving a space just big enough she could fit. Still fully dressed and donning her cloak, she climbed out of the bedroom window and settled herself on the edge of the roof. Her legs dangled over the edge as she looked down on Liph.

Not a single person could be seen this late at night. Not a soul dared to brave the cold. Only shadows. She wondered if her sister would send a servant to their parents with her warning. Would she force them to brave the brutal wind before the storm? Probably. Loralye never cared much for what anyone else felt. Certainly not the lower born.

Her hood blew back and a strong gust sent the strands of her hair flinging away from her face with it. She peered over the top of the buildings, out toward the water. The ocean. This time of night it was like an extension of the sky, broken up by tiny islands that dotted the surface. She watched the waves push and pull, unable to identify crests in the water but liking the way it broke up the constellations that reflected off it.

The N'skari were big into astronomy. The gods hadn't been seen or heard from in thousands of years, but they believed that they still spoke to us, just in different ways. To them, everything was fate, and despite the existence of Lady Fortuna, they did not believe in chance. What you were born as, you would die as. You never aspire to anything more than what the gods deemed you.

Quinn thought that interesting, given in the course of her not-so-long life, she'd been born a Maji and a highborn N'skari. She'd been sold into slavery and then earned her freedom. She'd been imprisoned multiple times, and each one she found her way free. She was now part of a noble House, but it wasn't the one she'd been born into, though she was beginning to think it might be the one she'd die in.

She peered up at the stars, and while the gods might look down on them, she thought it best not to try to interpret what they saw. Who was to say what was bad or good? Right or wrong? There were gods that had been deemed dark, just as there were ones that were seen as light. Ultimately, though, they were all gods—and she and the rest of the people in this world were all men. She remembered the one time she'd told one of the Sacred Sisters that taught the highborn children that. The lady had gone quiet and that night Quinn had gone to bed bruised and without dinner.

She didn't hear the knock on her door, but she felt the presence that drew near.

"Mind if I join you?" Draeven called out her window. Quinn motioned to the spot beside her with a wave of her hand. A few moments later he hauled himself out onto the steep ledge and took the spot at her side.

Within seconds his teeth were chattering. He wrapped the cloak tighter around himself.

"Come to pry for Lazarus?" she asked. Draeven scoffed.

"Please," he said. "Like I would climb out on this roof in these conditions for him." Quinn didn't turn, but she pressed her lips together.

"If he gave you the order, you would," she said. "You're a good vassal like that."

"I suppose you're right." He nodded, clenching his jaw tight to try to stop the chattering. "But to answer your question, no. I'm not here for him."

Quinn nodded, because she believed him. While annoyingly good and obnoxiously optimistic, Draeven was not a liar. At least to her.

"If not for him, then what has brought you out here?" she asked, pulling her own cloak tighter. She'd always loved to sit on the roof as a child, but she didn't remember it being quite this cold.

"Can't I just come sit with you because I feel like it?" he asked, his expression amused instead of affronted.

"I'm me and you're you," she said. "We exist as opposites for Lazarus. You, his left-hand that plays nice with others; and I his right, that would prefer stabbing them. What are you here for? I'm not buying that this is just an act of kindness." She pursed her lips and he sighed heavily.

"Very well," he nodded, dropping a smidgen of the Lord Sunshine attitude. "I came to ask if you know what you're doing."

Quinn's eyebrows drew together.

"Know what I'm doing?" she repeated, suspecting what he was getting at but not saying so.

"You've made it abundantly clear that Lazarus

was wrong in sailing into N'skara without being invited. That we would be dead without you, but I'm not an idiot, Quinn. You're planning something. I don't know what it is, or why, though I can guess it has something to do with your parents and sister." He looked away and exhaled heavily. "You understand these people, but you're playing with them as much as you play with us. We might be here for Lazarus to get an alliance, but you're only here for something else entirely. Aren't you?"

She didn't answer him at first, instead choosing to weigh her options.

Eventually she settled on the truth, or at least half of it.

"Not exactly," she said. "I want Lazarus to get his audience."

"But?" he prompted. She glowered a little.

"But I have unfinished business in my homeland," she said. It was as much as she would say on the subject.

"That's becoming quite obvious, though Lazarus is choosing to look the other way." Draeven exhaled and a cloud of white plumed in front of him before being caught in the wind. "He's a smart man," Draeven continued. "A logical man. It's why I chose to follow him. Why I do the things I do." He looked away, and she sensed there was more to it that he wasn't saying. "I knew he would be king one day, because Lazarus is one of the rare few in the world that makes himself. He doesn't allow circumstances or other people to define him, and while what he asks is great at times . . . I know that one day very soon it will all be worth it, because I'll be in a position to help those that need it most." He turned and stared at her with an unsettling intensity. "So, I ask you again, do you know what you're doing? Because if you don't, it isn't Lazarus that will pay the price, but the rest of us. He may not get his alliance, but I have no doubt he'd find a way to still become king. He will move on. All of our hopes and dreams, though, will die here in this land that you've both led us to."

Quinn swallowed, but she didn't look away. Draeven, while kind and occasionally funny and almost always too nice to everyone but her, was also brutally honest when he needed to be. It was ultimately what won her over and made her stop daydreaming about killing him. He had a way of being the most honest, and sometimes the most vulnerable, but it wasn't because he was a weak man. It was because he was strong. She respected him for it, more than she would ever say.

"I know what I'm doing," she whispered. "I promise."

He stared at her for another moment before nodding once. "Good," he said. "Because if you don't . . ." Draeven shook his head but she got the meaning.

Little did he know, it was a warning she didn't need. Quinn was painfully aware of what happened to those that crossed the N'skari.

And what would become of all of them should she fail.

Bastille in the Gateway

"Even in times of great joy, there can also be great sorrow—
for emotions are not so shallow as to be all or nothing."
— Quinn Darkova, vassal of House Fierté, fear twister,
white raksasa, second daughter of the Darkova Household

D raven left sometime later and she came back in, shutting the door and turning the lock to ensure that she remained undisturbed for the remainder of the night. Quinn ripped away her cloak and tossed it clear across the room. It landed in a heap beneath the window. Striding toward the bed, she fell—face first—down into its cushioned embrace. The distinct smell of dust rose up and tickled her nose. Whoever had lent the group this house had not been in it for some time. Even though she and the rest of Lazarus' party had been there for several nights, there was still a layer of grime that clung to every available surface.

Blinking against the mattress covers, Quinn groaned and leveraged herself up so that she could reach down and remove her boots as well, letting them fall from her hands with heavy *thunks* before she turned and rested back against the bed.

So tired, she thought briefly as the weight of her lethargy pulled her under. She had been more than awake before they left the Arvis House; she'd been ready to tear into Loralye—ready to bleed her if she must to get what she wanted. That energy had drained on the way back and drained further still while she sat out on the roof with Draeven. Her mind was not quiet, but her body demanded sleep. It felt as if something—or someone—was calling to her, dragging her toward the blessed nothingness. Her eyes fell shut and she began to drift . . .

The hard splash of cold water hit her with a shock. So chilled it contained sheets of ice, those frozen chips cut deep into her flesh. Quinn gasped as her eyes opened and she rose to her elbows, then bolted to her feet as she shook off the lingering drops. They started to freeze to her skin.

Quinn paused, her hand falling away from her side, where she had reached for her dagger—as she realized that once again she'd had been catapulted into the realm of dreams. Or more precisely, she'd been yanked from her own world and dropped unceremoniously before the same temple of the dark gods she had been led to during her last visit.

The place she'd seen just before the N'skari attacked their ship.

Quinn sucked in a breath as she lifted her chin and took in the statues of gods. They remained, but they'd also been changed since her last visit. Their eyes were now blackened like ash. They stared down at her with darkness in their gazes. She couldn't decide whether it was more inhuman or less than the white marble veined with streaks of gray.

Her feet carried her forward a step or two before she paused and saw the bird sitting on one of the spokes of the roof, observing her with a tilted head and mischievous glint in its eye. Quinn examined the creature with a mixture of wariness and confusion. It had led her here before and yet again, here it rested.

Before Quinn could think too deeply on the presence of the bird, the doors creaked open, a gray, muted light shining from within. She jerked, her hand going to her dagger and *yanking it from its sheath as the statue of Mazzulah moved. Its arm rose as the face of the statue turned. It pointed to the open doors. Whatever this place was, whatever the statues meant, it was clear she was meant to go inside.*

Quinn sheathed her dagger and took another step forward, following the gods urging as she ascended the steps. The doors widened further as she approached, and her heart began to thump heavily in her chest as a sense of foreboding fell over her. Blood rushed in her ears, the sound like a dull roar.

Inside, the temple was awash in smoke—a soft cloud-like substance clung to the walls and ceiling, making finding her way that much more difficult. Quinn squinted through the soft light, striding forward.

The further she walked, the clearer her surroundings became. Bars nearly two inches thick and twenty feet tall lined the long hall. Cages, tall and imposing. They were all empty, but the blood-stained floors and chains still attached to the walls said a great deal about what they'd been used for.

Quinn continued onward.

Feeling a pull to something unknown within this bastille for the depraved.

Then she heard it. The sound of claws scraping over the stone floors. Beasts moaning. Animals screaming. She couldn't place what they were or where they came from. Only that the sound surrounded her the further she walked. The closer she got.

Then she saw them. Inside the cages, no more than shadows of whatever they were or had been. The creatures were being held in the nether. Their bodies in one realm— their minds in another. As they were tortured, they drifted here, to the place between the human realm, the dark realm, and the realm of the gods. This was the Gateway.

Of course, it made sense now why she had not been able to reach it before. She hadn't been allowed. Someone from within must have sensed her, must have called her forth again.

Deep inside she knew that all of her searching had brought her here. That her determination, her conviction—it was a tether, pulling her in the direction she needed to go.

To the one she came back for.

Risk.

Quinn squinted through the smoke and curling tendrils of darkness that outlined her. It was the first line of defense, were something to come after her here in the in-between. She'd walked it many times, not without understanding what or where she was, or why when she woke that what happened in the dreams had been real.

Somehow, someway, perhaps some god had given her the ability to walk where no other could. All she knew was that she owed them a great debt when she found the cell that was calling to her.

Quinn knew by the spill of blood that flowed between the cracks in the marbled floors. Most blood looked the same, but this held a shade of blue within it. It was not completely human, but part raksasa.

"Risk?" Quinn reached out, gripping the bars of her sister's cell. A whimper escaped from beyond the other side. She called again, "Risk? Is that you?"

Soft breathing and then . . . "Go away."

Quinn blinked at the sharp bark that echoed back. There was no doubt in her mind that it was Risk, but she couldn't understand the vehement sound of her younger sister's voice. Quinn shook her head and pressed closer to the bars. "It's me; Quinn. Risk, where are you? I'm trying to find you."

"Stop it." Risk screamed before her voice dropped into a low deep moan. "Stop it . . . no more . . . stop. I will hear no more. Stop torturing me. She's not here. I don't want to hear her voice. I know she's not here."

Quinn's eyes widened as the figure moved closer, pacing the confines of her prison like a caged animal. The sound of chains dragging across a stone floor resounded up the interior. Quinn realized then that Risk didn't truly think she was there. She thought she was hearing her voice, but that it wasn't real.

Quinn didn't hesitate. Slamming her hands on the bars and letting the sound vibrate up toward the blurred ceiling to draw the girl's attention, she called through the barrier that separated them. "It's not an illusion, Risk. I'm here. Look this way." The slight movement beyond told her that the girl was following her instructions. Quinn had to take a moment not to let her excitement get the better of her. It would not be so simple. So easy. "Come closer," she commanded.

The creature's head turned back and forth. "No. Every time I do, you hurt me. I'm done. The next time I come to you, I will rip your throat out with my teeth. I'll do it, you know I can."

Quinn did know. She remembered quite clearly what she'd seen before, in the very first dream those months ago. How long had Risk been calling for her?

"It's me, Risk. I promise you. It's me. Come closer, I have to make sure it's you."

With a burst of speed, the creature within the confinement charged at the bars. Quinn released them a breath before the girl hurdled herself at them, teeth snapping, eyes flashing an iridescent blue in anger. Quinn felt her lips part in surprise. Ten years, she had to remind herself. It had been ten years since she had seen her sister. It was obvious Risk had felt every moment of those ten years.

Her hair, once the same silver that Quinn's had held, was a limp dull white. The strands hung around the girl's face in wet, ragged clumps. The only brightness in her eyes was drawn from the seething anger that raged within. Her skin, *once the color of ashes, was pallid and almost as white as her hair. Quinn wondered when she'd last seen the sun.*

If it had been ten years since that too.

Risk's nails were long and sharp, as if she'd been honing them on the stone walls into points that could stab through a man's jugular. The horns that she'd once hidden beneath her hair had outgrown any attempts at normalcy. They arched up, curling like a ram—elegant and darker than even the gray her skin should've been. Quinn felt her teeth grind at how malnourished she was. Her delicate frame was now pitifully frail, her stomach more than sunken in. Risk was a living, breathing skeleton.

An ice-cold violence rose within Quinn. She would make whoever did this pay.

"Risk," Quinn said. "I need you to tell me where you are."

Risk's own expression had dulled upon seeing Quinn's figure. She hadn't realized it, but just as she had examined her younger sister, Risk had been staring at her. The girl blinked, her eyes large and practically bulbous in her skinny face. She was all sharp angles—skin stretched over bone with nothing beneath.

"It's really you," she breathed, her voice barely above a whisper.

Quinn nodded. "Yes, I told you. Now, I need you to help

me so I can help you. Tell me where you are. I need to find you."

Risk shook her head, the movement slow. "I don't know . . . I've been here for so long. I don't . . ." she trailed off, her head turning as another noise sounded—from deeper within the cage.

"Risk!" Quinn called her back. "Don't lose focus. Try to think. What was the last thing you remember?"

"I don't know how long since I was brought here," Risk admitted. "You disappeared and then . . ."

Quinn waited, but impatience won out. She could feel Risk drifting away even though the girl never moved. "Give me something. Anything. Who took you? What was the last thing you saw? What do you see now?"

"This isn't real . . ." she heard her say. "It's just my mind. I've fallen asleep. I need to wake up now. I don't want to. It hurts when I'm awake."

"I'm coming for you," Quinn promised, the air sliding between her clenched teeth as she thought of all of the ways she would torture those responsible for this. "Never doubt that, Sister. I will come for you. I just need your help."

"No, you can't come," Risk said. "I'm supposed to be here. I'm meant to be here. Unnatural, evil, inhuman things belong in the dark, Quinn. I am all three."

Not nearly as much as Quinn, herself, was—she knew.

But it was clear that wherever Risk was—whoever was holding her had trained her to believe that.

Believe herself evil, just for her blood.

"Sometimes beasts must be contained for the greater good," Risk said, her voice wavering as the noise beyond her grew louder. Someone was waking her up. Quinn couldn't let that happen, but the words coming from her sister's lips gave her pause.

"What did you say?" Quinn asked.

"Creatures of the darkness must be contained," she repeated. "It's for the greater good. I must be chained. Taught my place in the world." She paused, air whistling in her lungs, expanding her chest as though it were an inflating sail. "This is my place." The words were rote. They sounded foreign on her own lips—as if someone were speaking through her. With a start, Quinn recalled whose mouth they had come from.

Her blood turned icy as Risk looked back, her blue eyes —so like Quinn's own—dull with resignation when before, her anger had allowed her a modicum of life. "I have to go."

Quinn wanted to call out, to stop her, but before she could shake off the wave of rage that filled her, Risk was gone. Her cage empty. The fog cleared away and the gate that must have held it closed was unlocked by unseen hands, swinging inward.

She stepped forward, her booted feet sliding in Risk's blue blood. Only feet away from her lay cruel chains, the kind one might use on a rabid animal. They were covered in blood. Quinn committed the sight to memory. She would recall them when she found those responsible.

Before the end of her time in N'skara—Quinn would ensure that someone else's blood ran in rivers over the stones of this temple.

Unforgiving Waters

"We must take care with what we put out into the world, for one day the gods will give it back."
— *Quinn Darkova, vassal of House Fierté, fear twister, white raksasa, second daughter of the Darkova Household, kidnapper*

Her steps were as silent as the wind was loud.

The storm on the horizon was near, and with it, freezing blasts of air and water whipped through the alleyways. Quinn's fingers, already numb from emotion, clenched the hem of her cloak tight to keep the hood from falling back.

Across the street from her, a man walked

about, clad in white robes—unknowing to the woman that stalked him. She followed after, thankful for the blustery winds, blowing snow over her footprints. She could be as silent as she liked, but those would be far more damning with what she planned to do.

The man turned a corner, going deeper into the city, further away from both her own accommodations and his mansion. This was the poorer part of Liph, home to most of the lower born, those not lucky enough to have some magic that would afford them servitude instead of poverty. Quinn's eyebrows drew together, the corner of her lips turning down as she followed after.

The streets were devoid of people, only a straggler here or there, likely because crime was far more prominent—not that it was ever reported. The N'skari didn't care what happened in the dregs of their society. It was only in the pristine parts of life, where the statues of light gods followed every move, that they attempted to appear as just and pure as the robes they wore.

The man's white robes stood out stark in comparison to the dingy gray of the buildings that matched that of the slushed snow in the streets. He wrinkled his nose, taking another turn down an alley so tiny and silent that even the roar of the wind was a faraway thing.

Quinn picked up her pace, her quality boots built near as well for the snow as that of the N'skari. The snow crunched as he slinked between two buildings and Quinn came up behind him, holding the wooden staff in its compressed form. She swung once, slamming the end into the side of his head.

A crack echoed.

He collapsed.

Sprawled and lifeless in the path, his white robes ran gray with streaks of black from the grime that festered and thrived in the corners of the houses. No one came out to see what the noise was, and she knew they wouldn't. Not a word would reach the Council until it was too late. Her plan would already be in motion.

But first, she needed to get him to the water.

Casting a glower down at the unconscious prick, she grabbed the back of his robes, fisting as much of the fabric as she could, and began pulling. He was both heavier and less so than she expected. Her Maji strength made moving him possible, but the water seeping into his hair and clothes added more weight she hadn't wanted to carry. She looked down, her brow furrowing. Where she needed to go was several streets away, but mostly downhill.

She pivoted on foot and started to drag him through the streets. If any looked upon her, they would see him, and only him walking toward the pier—which made the lower born look away for fear of being scolded, or worse. It worked in her favor and anytime they came across someone. The path was almost instantly cleared to make way for the councillor that they did not know was unconscious.

Quinn let out an umph, shaking her head in disgust when she got to the edge of the city where rocks separated the streets of Liph from the gray sand beaches. The ashwood pier was the only way out to the water. Quinn looked down at the man and then to the pier beyond, what she planned to do was as wicked as it was cruel.

He deserves nothing less for what he's done. All of them do.

With that thought, she pulled him onto the wooden dock and dragged him to the very end. The waters churned anxiously, lending credence to what she was about to do. Quinn smirked to herself and started to pull the stones from her pockets. She dumped them on the deck beside her and then carefully loaded them in the folds of his robe—careful not to wake him.

She needed him to sleep for just a little longer.

Casting a glance over the empty pier, she looked out into the distance, where fishermen and the city's guard were patrolling the waters. Lazarus' ship stood out stark among the N'skari boats, its black sails and dark ebony wood striking against the pale, muted land and sea around it.

None looked her way, not that it would matter if they did. She took a deep breath before kneeling down and reaching for the icy waters. She scooped a handful, flinging it to the side. It splashed her captive in the face, and he spluttered awake.

"What in the—where—" His words caught in his throat upon seeing her.

"Hello, Edward," she greeted.

Fear, deep and true, stirred within him, adding fuel to an already too hot flame. She grinned, pacing in circles around him.

"What have you done?" he demanded. She thought it an interesting question.

"So far?" she asked with an air of nonchalance. "Nothing much. I knocked you unconscious and brought you here." She motioned to the choppy sea, and Edward swallowed.

Her sister was right, at least in one thing. Quinn did love her twisted games.

"And what exactly do you think you can do?" he asked, sitting up completely, glaring at her. "The Council will come looking for me and when they do, I'll tell them of your treachery. I'll tell them—"

Quinn clenched her hand and his words stopped short as he choked on his fear. Her blood pumped as his panic rose, the scent of damp petals and snow in the air.

"Nothing," she whispered. "You'll tell them nothing, because dead men tell no tales."

She smiled as his face completely blanched of what little color it had. The sopping silver strands of his long hair clung to parts of his face, droplets of water falling, scattering around him both from his trembling and the wind.

"You won't get away with this," he said, swallowing hard when she continued to grin, completely unperturbed.

"Actually," she said. "I will. If anyone looks this way, they'll see you standing alone on a pier—looking very thoughtfully into those waters. They may or may not see you jump, but either way, by the time your body is found, it will be too late. You really shouldn't have provoked me at dinner last night, Edward." She leaned down, cupping his cheek. He jerked away and she let out a laugh. "I told you that Ramiel's guidance wouldn't be merciful. You should have listened."

His fingers curled as he started to back away. Edward was a passion cleaver but a weak one. He struggled to use his ability under pressure when they were children, and while her blood cooled a fraction, stolen away as he tried to suck all of the rising excitement in her veins, it wasn't near enough to stop what she was about to do. He couldn't rip her emotions away any more than he could get away.

She'd find it sad, if the icy rage inside her didn't run so deep.

"What do you want?" he asked, his voice rising as it warbled. "Money? J-jewels? It's all yours, just don't—"

She grabbed him by the hem of his robe, pulling him up so that their faces were only inches apart.

"Where is Risk?" she asked.

"R-risk?" he stuttered as he repeated the name, trying for confusion. She saw guilt in his face, and Quinn gritted her teeth.

"Mariska Darkova," she spat. "She has gray

skin, horns, skinny as a waif, eyes of an N'skari—where is she? Where are you keeping her?" she demanded the truth from him even as she kept her voice steady and low. A deadly sort of calm had taken her, and it wouldn't be long before she'd dance with Mazzulah. She'd let the god of the dark realm infest her soul and drive her to the brink of insanity—if it got her what she came for.

"I-I don't kn-know what y-y-you're—"

"Talking about?" she said. "Wasn't it you who, just yesterday, was telling me that some beasts need to be contained, caged, to be taught their place in the world?"

Silence.

She lifted an eyebrow and Edward didn't deny it. He knew death was coming for him, and yet still he tried to stop it.

"I-I didn't do it—I swear—w-whatever you've heard, I didn't d-do it—"

She rose to her feet, pulling him up with her. His legs scrambled as he tried to find his footing. She didn't award him that grace as she grabbed onto one wooden post with her free hand and extended him over the waters with the other.

"Where is she?" Quinn asked again.

"They locked her up," he said. "I didn't do it—"

"Locked her up," Quinn repeated, interrupting his useless pleas. "Locked her up where?"

"I'll tell you if you let me go," he said, attempting to bargain with death.

Quinn's lips didn't twitch as she said, "Tell me where, and I'll let you go."

"You swear on the gods?" he asked. Her arm started to shake. She wouldn't be able to hold him like this much longer.

"I swear it," she answered. "Now, where is she?"

Edward didn't realize that his words were less what she wanted than his thoughts. His memories. Fear rode him in the face of pressure and as he gave her half-attempted answers, she saw the gaps in his mind. "Go through the lowborn side of Liph and turn w-west. At the edge of the city there's a p-path."

"How will I know it?" she asked.

"There's a lantern. It's meant to w-ward off those who don't kn-know the path is th-there." In his mind a silver cage hung from a sycamore tree, and inside a candle was lit, imbued with the magic he spoke of.

"I see," Quinn said.

Her fingers unclenched and his robe slipped from them. The look of shock on his face was near priceless as he fell toward the icy waters. His back hit them with a splash, but Edward was a strong swimmer despite the rocks. He reached for the dock, clawing at the waves with all his might.

"You s-swore," he yelled, teeth chattering.

Quinn squatted down but made no move to reach for him. "I swore to let you go and I did. You were the one that never specified where."

Outrage and terror flashed in his eyes as he clawed aimlessly toward the dock. His fingers brushed the wood pillar that might have let him live. Quinn tsked.

"Uh uh," she wagged her finger, pulling on the tendrils of fear inside him and stirring them into a frenzy. He started to scream, and the waves poured into his mouth. That scream turned into a warbled choke as the tide grabbed onto him and pulled.

Several moments of silence passed where Quinn stood on the end of the peer and waited.

The sun rose in the sky, peeking through the heavy clouds in rays, and still the silence held.

When Edward Arvis surfaced no more, Quinn turned on her heel and started for the west side of the city.

She'd killed a man, but she felt no guilt. No shame.

It was her first kill. The first piece of retribution meted.

The only last words she would give him were a whisper on the sea as she said, "You shall reap what you sow."

They all will.

Mazzulah's Temple

"Some evil is so dark that there is no atonement. Only Beliphor's embrace."
— *Quinn Darkova, vassal of House Fierté, fear twister,*
white raksasa, second daughter of the Darkova Household,
unrepentant murderess

Q uinn climbed the stone steps—there had to be a thousand of them—but she did it, and she did it before nightfall. Despite the cold sweat that soaked her clothes and slicked over her skin, she didn't dare remove the cloak, not this far from where she was supposed to be. She hadn't seen a soul since she dropped Edward in the sea, and she wondered if that was Fortuna's favor or simply happenstance. Either way, it was a long walk up. As Quinn came to the very last step and looked past the craggy branches and dead leaves, a plateau spanned out before her.

Marble statues with blackened eyes greeted her. It was the gods that the N'skari had deemed as too dark and corrupt. Among them, Mazzulah was the largest and the only one well kept. Neither a man nor a woman, but somehow both, the statue seemed to glow with an inner light, just as those blackened eyes seemed to burnish darkness. The others had been left to fare against the elements. Vines covered their pedestals and fallen branches their names, but Quinn knew them from her dreams.

Just as she knew the temple that rose up behind them.

It was a work of dark beauty built by some ancient people, long before N'skara picked and chose which deities to follow. It was smaller relative to most temples, but Quinn knew that in its prime, it would have been far more opulent—for even the ruins held a certain air of otherworldliness that demanded her attention.

"Which house are you from?" The voice pulled her attention to the obsidian double doors, where two guards stood dressed in white. Quinn kept her hood drawn as her fingers wrapped around the hilt of her knife, pulling it from under her shirt but keeping it hidden in the folds of her cloak as she approached.

"I'm here for the prisoner," Quinn said, mimicking Loralye's bored tone from the night before.

"It's House Arvis' turn today," the guard said.

Turn? Turn for what?

A sick feeling settled in her gut. Had Edward been coming here when she followed him? If so, what exactly had he been intending to do?

A stone settled in her stomach as the other guard repeated, "Which House are you from?"

Quinn drew back the hood of her cloak, and they both gasped, lunging for their weapons.

She slashed out in a wide arc, cutting them both across the middle. Red splattered her boots as they both dropped to their knees. Spinning, Quinn plunged the knife in her palm through the eye of one of the guards. He didn't even make a sound as she yanked the blade out, pushing against his shoulder. Instead, his face—frozen in shock—hit the cold hard ground as he bled out. Dead.

"What, exactly, was House Arvis meant to do today?" Quinn asked the remaining guard. The man held his stomach with both hands, but crimson seeped through his robes.

"I don't know—I'm just a guard," he sobbed, tears running down his cheeks.

"Tell me what it was his turn to do, and I'll make it quick," she said. Quinn held up the knife, and the blade glistened red. She liked it that way, though the guard, if he could be called that, looked like he was going to be sick.

"The councillors take their turns visiting her. They say she's the cause of their darkness," he breathed. Quinn lifted the tip of the blade to his chin, drawing his gaze up.

"What do they take turns doing?" she asked again, needing to know. Having to understand what exactly had taken place here.

"Because she tempts them, they take their pleasure in her," he whispered. Quinn grit her teeth. She didn't have time for this. She lifted a free hand to his face and sent tendrils of fear into him.

What she saw made her stomach turn.

Rape. Again and again and again. It was endless. It was all she saw. Face after face passed her by, but at the end of every visit was a naked girl on the marble floors bleeding as seed leaked from her.

They used and abused her for as long as this guard knew.

He'd been guard at the temple six years and not once had they missed a day.

The boy, whoever he was, knew what was coming but true to her word she made it quick. The blade slashed through the flesh of his neck without resistance. He gurgled for a moment before toppling sideways and falling silent.

Quinn rested one bloody hand on the door and paused.

Take their pleasure in her . . . she shook her head, wishing she'd have drawn out Edward's death. He had been coming here to rape her.

That dream from many nights long gone now made sense.

Quinn swallowed hard, a burn in her throat as her gaze swept up on their own accord. There on the sloping roof, sat a black bird watching her. A shudder ran through Quinn, because it was indeed the work of some god that brought her here today. Whatever their reasons, Mazzulah wanted her to find Risk.

Quinn wasn't going to keep her waiting.

She pushed on the door and it swung open. There was no gray light. No smoke. The cages that lined the long hall were still there though, and at the very end she heard it.

Chains scraping the floor. The quiet hiss of something gone feral.

Quinn strode forward, her feet picking up speed as she saw the guard in white. He looked her over and squinted. "Loralye Arvis?" he asked.

Quinn raised her hand, and the metal gleamed in the low light. "Think again," she replied softly. Her arm rotated back as she snapped her wrist forward and threw. The knife spun wildly for all of a second before planting itself in his heart. The blade he held in his hand clattered to the floor as he stumbled.

She approached, pulling the blade from his chest to slide it over his throat. Crimson ran and Quinn turned her back on the sounds of him gagging as she stowed her blade, looking into the cage.

Huddled in the corner, it was hard to make out the figure inside, but Quinn knew it to be her sister.

Her true sister. Risk.

She reached for the bars. Her fingers wrapped around them, stiff but slippery from blood.

"I came for you, Risk," Quinn whispered. The tiny body lifted its head from its knees. Two gleaming horns of onyx rose up as the girl opened her eyes and the most iridescent blue she'd ever seen stared back.

"Quinn . . ." The name slipped past her lips, awe and hesitation in her broken, raw voice. "Is it really you?" she asked, the words hopeful, but at the same time afraid to give life to that hope. After all she'd learned this eve, Quinn understood why. She might have been a slave, but Risk had endured other horrific things in the times they'd been parted.

"It's really me," Quinn nodded. "I'm going to take you away from here."

Her sister shuffled forward on her hands and knees. Large manacles surrounding her wrists and ankles. Quinn grimaced. Her hands clenched the bars as she shook them, and the door swung open without resistance. Metal hinges creaked as she stumbled forward, but Quinn didn't pay it any mind. She dropped onto her knees before the person she'd traveled over strange lands and dark seas to find. The only person, whose very existence helped her get through the many years living in such an awful, terrible place.

"I can't believe it," Risk whispered, reaching a tentative shaking hand for her. "They told me you'd been sold. That you were never coming back."

Quinn held out her palm. Their fingers touched. Even after all these years, their hands were still the same size.

"They didn't think I would," Quinn answered back. "But nothing could keep me from coming back for you." The first makings of a smile shined on her younger sister's face, but it quivered before falling into a flat line.

Risk lifted both arms.

"I can't run, Quinn. There is no key." She looked them over, noticing how the ones at her wrist and ankles connected together and then to the wall. "Even if I could run, I'm too weak. I can barely move."

Quinn shook her head. "I'll carry you if I have to, but you're not staying here any longer for them to—" Her words died in her throat as Risk started to tremble.

"Don't say it," Risk asked. Demanded. Quinn lowered her head and focused on the chains, pushing the other thoughts from her mind. The ones that urged her to do equally terrible things to the ones that harmed her younger sister. Those thoughts wouldn't help her right now.

"Alright," she inched forward slowly. "I think I can get these off, but I'm going to have to touch you." She didn't phrase it like a question, but Risk understood. She shuffled forward, closer, meeting her in the middle, and extended both arms before her.

"Do it," Risk whispered. "Please."

Quinn nodded. She pulled the dagger, still sticky with blood, and angled the tip to slip it into the thin slit where a key should fit. Metal grinded against metal as she pressed hard, holding her sister's wrist in one hand as gently as possible. If Risk felt any pain or trepidation about Quinn's touch, she didn't show it.

The blade scraped down the side of the locking mechanism. She jiggled it twice and the lock clicked. The manacle opened and fell to the floor with a clang.

She glanced up at Risk's wide eyes as her sister's stared at her bare wrist for what Quinn had to guess was the first time in years. The skin was scarred over but inflamed. White lines marred her flesh where the metal had bit in time and time again. Quinn kept her anger under control as she gently took the other hand and started to work on that manacle.

"You still pick locks," Risk rasped as her other arm was freed. Quinn nodded, helping her settle back so she could pull her ankle up into the dim light.

"I've gotten quite a bit better at it," Quinn replied. Slipping the blade into the bigger opening. This one came free almost instantly.

"You've graduated from using hair pins to knives. When did that happen?" Risk asked, trying to lift her other leg into Quinn's lap. She shook from the exertion and it took all of Quinn's willpower not to grimace. She delicately grasped her other ankle and pulled it up, jamming the blade into the opening. She had to try it twice just to find the slit.

"I was sold into slavery. One of the boys on a large farm I worked on came from a blacksmith family. He understood locks and I understood words. I taught him Norcastan and he helped me become proficient enough with the blade to break most any lock." As if on cue, the final cuff clicked as it opened, and the metal dropped into the pile between them. Tentatively Quinn lowered her ankle to the ground and stood to hold out both hands.

Risk grasped them, and with great effort managed to pull herself to her feet. If Quinn had to guess, it was the first time she'd stood without chains in years.

She took several steps in a circle, her head shaking but a smile on her face. "I can still walk," she murmured as if she was afraid that she might not have been able to again.

Quinn's heart might have broken at that, if not for the subtle fury that was building. She stored her knife and reached for the ties of her cloak. Risk tilted her head, squinting. Realization dawned on her when Quinn pulled it free and extended it to her.

Risk lifted a hand, grasping the thick fabric in her fingers. She pulled it close, tucking it around her as Quinn had, and fumbling on the ties. Quinn reached up to help her and she flinched.

Quinn paused.

"I'm sorry," Risk whispered hoarsely. "I—"

"It's okay," Quinn said. They stared at each other for a moment, and a look of understanding passed. "I've been there before. I still don't enjoy most people's touch." Risk swallowed, but didn't say anything. Quinn extended a hand again and asked, "Can I help you?"

The younger girl nodded.

With bloodstained hands she reached for her sister and tied the cloak shut to keep away most of the chill and conceal her naked body. Risk lowered her head, as if she were still a servant, but in truth she'd been treated more as a pleasure slave for quite a long time.

Quinn stepped back and opened the cell door. Risk took several tentative steps forward before faltering. Quinn lunged after her, letting the door swing shut—clanging loudly—as she scrambled to grab her before she hit the floor. There was no one to hear the noise, though. At least, she didn't think so. Quinn turned her attention back to Risk. Given how painfully skinny she was, Quinn worried she might break if she fell or stumbled again.

Risk let out a hiss, not in fear or hate, but of pain.

"I'm not going to be able to walk out of here," she said in a hush.

Quinn rebalanced her on her feet, but kept an arm around her waist. "Then I'll carry you."

"But won't the guards—"

"The guards are dead," she replied. "And if we run into more, those ones will follow them into the dark realm as well."

She waited to see how her sister responded to the harsh reality that the twisted girl she'd known had grown up to be a killer. Risk didn't seem bothered by it much, if at all.

"How will you fight them if you're holding me?" she asked.

"I have ways," Quinn replied.

Fear is more deadly than the blade upon her hip, but it was probably best not to mention that just yet.

"Alright," Risk answered. She turned into her and reached up, wrapping both her fragile arms around Quinn's neck. She leaned in, taking care to angle her head so her horns did not stab Quinn, and whispered, "Please don't drop me."

"I won't," she answered. "I promise."

Quinn knew she shouldn't make promises, but nothing and no one—not even Lazarus—was going to part them again. She leaned forward and wrapped one arm around her back, the other around her knees as she picked her up with ease. Quinn held her to her chest and walked out of Mazzulah's temple.

Somewhere in the distance a bird cawed.

A single silver feather fluttered on the breeze but this time it was heading south. Quinn took that as all the answer she needed. Even from the dark realm, Mazzulah was there with them, watching Risk—and Quinn didn't question how or why. That bird was most certainly something from beyond the gate.

But the message was clear.

When she was done in N'skara, she would take Risk south.

Take her anywhere, so long as it was away from here.

All for Risk

"Sometimes blessings come in unlikely forms. The gods amuse
themselves that way."
— Quinn Darkova, vassal of House Fierté, fear twister,
white raksasa, second daughter of the Darkova Household,
repeated murderess

Cold, clammy fingers clenched around
Quinn's shoulders as she hefted Risk up
closer to her chest. Without the information she'd
gleaned from Edward or the dreams that had
plagued her, Quinn knew she would have never
found her sister. The accommodations she and the
others had been given was as far away as possible

from where Risk had been, without them being removed from the capital altogether.

Risk's soft pants echoed in her ear as Quinn paused at a bend, glancing around the corner to ensure the streets were still empty. Thankfully, they were. Pushing off from the building, Quinn hurried across the pathway and down the next alley.

"Quinn . . ." Risk's voice was weak, in pain.

"We're almost there," Quinn promised.

And they were. As soon as she cleared the next street, the house they were staying at came into view. She sped up toward it, keeping Risk's body as close to her own as possible, hoping to alleviate any jostling movement that might cause her further pain or harm. Quinn pulled up short on the back porch, but before she could ask, Risk reached over and unlatched the door.

Shooting her sister a quick look of thanks, Quinn shoved the door open with her booted foot, moved inside, and closed it with a kick. She rushed up the stairs, noting that the first floor was empty, but the sound of voices echoing from somewhere else in the house told her that at least a few of the others were still awake. Quinn didn't pause, but went immediately to her own chamber—she and

Risk performing the same routine until they were securely inside the safety of the room.

Setting Risk down gently on her feet, Quinn reached for the ties on the cloak. Risk jerked sharply, shying away from the touch, and Quinn froze, cursing herself internally. Before her sister could apologize needlessly again, Quinn shook her head and nudged her with a light gesture toward the single bed against the wall.

"Can you make it to the bed on your own?" Quinn asked. "Or—"

"Yes," Risk interrupted, shuffling forward on her bare feet. "I can make it." And then, in a much quieter, but firmer voice, she whispered, "I *will* make it."

Quinn stepped back and stood sentry as she moved across the floor, her feet sliding against the wood until she found the edge of the bed, turned and collapsed upon it. Once seated, Quinn went around the room, reaching for the water basin in the corner and pouring the once heated—now cold —water from the jug next to it into the bowl. Grabbing up the square cloth hanging over the side, Quinn dropped it into the water and turned, carrying the whole of it back across the room until she was at Risk's side.

Quinn went to her knees before the parted folds of the cloak that still hung on Risk's shoulders down to her calves. Reaching for the cloth in the water, Quinn rung it out and looked up at her sister, seeking permission. Risk swallowed and nodded her consent as Quinn began to clean her feet and legs.

"How long has it been?" Risk asked as the cloth rubbed over the top of one foot, wiping away what looked to be a decade of grime and filth.

"Ten years," Quinn replied.

"Ten years . . ." Risk repeated, echoing her surprise. "So long," she said. "I don't even know all the places you must have gone . . . things that must have happened."

Moving to the other foot, Quinn shrugged even as her lips turned down in a frown. Risk's face tightened. She was in pain and from the way Quinn's insides churned at the taste of fear in the air, her sister wasn't as calm as she tried to appear.

"I've been a lot of places, seen and done a lot of things," Quinn replied. "And now . . ." She rubbed the cloth up Risk's leg—eliciting a shiver and flinch again as she uncovered a particularly dark bruise that made her clench her teeth and move away, dropping the cloth back into the water before wringing it out once more. "Now you'll be able to do the same," she finished.

"I think I can manage now," Risk said quietly, reaching for the cloth.

She turned away, hiding herself even as she tried to clean away the top layer of dirt from her skin. Biting down on the questions brimming in her mind, Quinn got to her feet and left the basin of water next to her. "I'll be right back," she said, heading for the door.

Risk's head jerked up, her eyes widening, but Quinn was already slipping into the hallway. She ran down the stairs, grateful that she had yet to bump into any of the others as she did so. Quinn snatched a half a loaf of bread and a dappa fruit from the kitchen before she sprinted back to the room. As she approached, the latch lifted and fell, and lifted and fell. Quinn paused and reached for it, opening the door as Risk had apparently been trying to do. Startled, Risk reared back, hissing—her eyes shining an even brighter blue—as she prepared to attack.

"It's me," Quinn said quickly, raising her hands up in a placating manner. "I just went to get you some food."

It took a moment, but Risk slowly stepped back

and straightened as much as she was able. "I-I'm sorry," she said, glancing away and focusing her attention on the floor. More fear erupted from the girl, and instead of enticing, the feel of it filling the room was actually stifling for a change.

Quinn frowned. "I was only gone for a moment," she said, trying to sound tender though it was a rough imitation. "I wouldn't leave you; I promise." Even the assurance fell flat. By the look of some of Risk's wounds, she *would* have to leave again, if only to find medicine. She didn't know how long some of those wounds—the bruises and cuts—had remained untreated too. She would need to run out to get something for them tonight or risk someone asking questions she couldn't yet answer if she went the next day.

Quinn contemplated all of this as Risk finished washing. As soon as she was done with as much as she could reach, Quinn reached out, not touching but quietly asking. Risk handed the cloth back before reaching up—her hands shaking with the effort of her movements—to untie the cloak and let it fall from her shoulders. Bending to pick up the basin, now full of water the color of sand, Quinn moved away and put it back upon the vanity she had gotten it from. She took her large long-sleeve sleep shirt and a pair of pants stolen from the drawer and silently handed them over to Risk, giving her a chance to dress.

"Why don't you—" Quinn stopped as she turned and found that Risk had seen the food she'd left behind and fallen upon it like a starving mad animal. Chest clenching in silent fury, Quinn took in the violence with which Risk tore at the bread with her fingers, shoving it in as quickly as she could lest someone come along to take the crumbs from her. When every spec of the loaf was gone, she snatched up the dappa fruit and bit into the outer skin. Red juices slid down her face, dripping from her chin as she chewed, swallowed, and bit again. After a moment, she paused, halfway through with the fruit, and her lips turned down in a grimace. "What's wrong?" Quinn asked as Risk put a hand to her stomach.

"I don't feel good," she admitted, dropping the fruit.

After having been starved into near extinction, she had tried to consume too much too fast, Quinn realized belatedly. Moving forward, she helped Risk to lift her legs so that she was fully on the bed even as she urged the girl to recline.

"Lay down," Quinn commanded. "I'm going to

run out for some medicine. The door will be locked and I—"

"No!" Risk shouted, her hand snapping out, fingers encircling Quinn's wrist as if her weak grip would keep her from going. "Don't leave."

Shocked by the power behind Risk's plea and the sharp acrid scent of fear wafting from her that strengthened in one powerful punch, Quinn blinked. "It will only be for a little bit," she tried to assure her sister. "I have to go get you some medicine."

Risk shook her head vehemently. "Please," she said, biting the word out even as she beseeched Quinn with her eyes. "Don't go."

Quinn was torn. She knew Risk would need the medicine even if she didn't go tonight, it was better to get it and be done with it. As she contemplated what to do, the soft sound of footsteps in the hallway reached her ears. Quinn stiffened when there was a soft knock on the door and Risk's grip on her wrist tightened.

"Quinn?" Lorraine's voice filtered through the wood. "Are you still up? When did you get back? Did you have dinner?"

"Who is that?" Risk hissed, suspicion and fear in her tone.

The answer to my problem. She thanked the gods as she extracted her arm from Risk's hand. "She's a friend," Quinn promised. "Just a moment. She won't hurt you; I swear it."

Striding across the room to the door, Quinn cracked it and peered out. She was blessedly relieved to find Lorraine standing there without her usual shadow behind her and took a moment to extend her field of vision, but Dominicus was not hovering anywhere else either.

"Quinn?" Lorraine looked surprised as she glanced down at her dirty, bloodstained, and water-soaked clothes. "What in the dark realm . . ."

Quinn didn't let her finish that statement, but lurched forward, grabbed the woman's hand, and yanked her inside, closing the door shut behind her as she did. "Lorraine, I need you to do me a favor," Quinn said quickly, dropping her hand.

Lorraine wasn't listening, however. Her gaze had strayed to the dark, ash skinned, horned girl huddling on the bed against the wall. "Quinn . . ." Lorraine breathed the name as she soaked in the girl's skeletal form beneath the oversized clothing. She jerked when Quinn reached forward and grabbed the woman's arm to steer her attention back in place.

"I need your help," Quinn said. "I need you to go out and get medicine. Something for cuts and bruises."

"Who—" Lorraine started before Quinn raised a finger and pressed it to the older woman's lips.

"And," Quinn said with meaning, "I need you to not ask any questions yet." She let her finger fall away. "I need the medicine first."

Lorraine frowned, her attention shifting from Quinn's hard face to the shuddering figure beyond. She nodded, slowly at first and then firmer as she made the internal decision to trust her. "Alright, I can go and be back in under the turn of an hour," Lorraine said. "But I'll need you to write it down. I doubt the N'skari will understand me."

Relief coursed through Quinn's veins and she pulled out a piece of parchment from the desk and scrawled in sloppy but legible words what she needed. She lifted the paper and blew on it twice, ensuring the ink dried quickly before turning it over and scrawling a haphazard map from here to the nearest physician she knew of.

"Make sure they do not keep this," Quinn said solemnly. "It must be burned, or it can be used as proof."

"Proof of what?" Lorraine asked.

Quinn rolled her shoulders back as she handed her the parchment.

There was no going back now.

"Treason."

Quinn opened the door to the room once more, urging the woman out. With a glance back, Lorraine said, "I'll return shortly."

She stepped back and shut the door completely, turning and resting her back against it wearily. She didn't want to admit it, but she was rather grateful in this moment for Lady Manners and her constant attempts at including Quinn and checking on her. Had she not come when she had . . . Quinn didn't want to think about what kind of fear-driven temper Risk might have fallen into. Her sister was on the edge of dancing with Mazzulah, judging by the wild look on her face as she stared at Quinn from across the room.

Shoving away from the door, Quinn approached her slowly. "Hey," she said, keeping her tone even. "It's alright. I don't have to leave now. Lorraine is going to go and get the medicine. I don't have to go anywhere. I'm all yours. I'm right here."

"Who was that woman?" Risk demanded, her voice cracking.

"She's a friend," Quinn reiterated, but still, Risk didn't appear to calm.

Quinn and she faced off, both of them unsure of the other and yet while one wanted to help—craved it as she never had before—and the other wanted to let her, neither of them let themselves step over that invisible line that had been drawn between them. The temporary relief of finding each other had stalled out into an uncomfortable hesitation. Quinn didn't want to scare Risk any more than she already had been, and it was more than presently clear that Risk couldn't seem to step away from the feeling that she'd be attacked or hurt at any moment that had been ingrained in her for years.

It was a long wait for Lorraine's return. When she did, knocking lightly, Quinn reached out to unlatch the door, palm facing Risk as if she were warding off a wild animal. Lorraine slid into the interior of the room, a small satchel in her hands as her attention darted to Risk and then back to Quinn.

She handed the bag over. "I got everything you requested," Lorraine said. "And already burned the parchment in the fireplace downstairs."

"Thank you," Quinn said and wasn't surprised

to feel that she meant it. She didn't like the idea of relying on others, but in this instance, she appreciated Lorraine's presence. Turning back to her sister, Quinn rifled through the bag and found the salve meant for bruises and cuts. She pulled the small circular jar from inside, popped the lid, and then flinched back at the smell. Pausing, she glanced between the opened container and Risk—who couldn't seem to tear her fixation away from Lorraine. *Perhaps it'd be better if Risk was asleep for the rest of this,* she thought. Quinn retrieved the dried lavender and valerian root, but paused when she realized it would need to be steeped in something for Risk to consume. Grimacing, she turned back to Lorraine only to have the herbs drawn from her hand by the older woman without any urging.

Lorraine sighed. "I'll make a tea," she said quietly, taking the lavender and valerian and disappearing from the room.

Sighing, Quinn set the bag on the nightstand and returned to Risk's side with the jar of salve. "Here, this will help with the pain and speed up the healing," she said, setting the jar down. "Do you want me to apply it or would you like to do it?"

"I can," Risk said wearily as she leaned forward, dipping her fingers into the yellowed substance that smelled of something rancid. She flinched as she applied the balm to her skin, rubbing it up her arms and over her stomach in long streaks.

By the time Lorraine returned with a small tray that held a single cup of tea, Risk's skin, or at least what was visible of it, shined with a strangely tinted hue that made her appear almost a peach tone. The salve began to dry as Quinn helped Risk lay back down, the younger girl's eyelids fluttering weakly despite Lorraine's presence.

"Drink this," Quinn urged, taking the cup from Lorraine. Risk shook her head, but Quinn would not be dissuaded. "You must," she said, lifting the girl's head and putting the rim of the cup to her lips. With flashing eyes that belied her physical weakness, Risk downed half of the tea before she sighed and turned away. "No, you have to drink all of it," Quinn ordered.

"Tyrant," Risk muttered as Quinn shoved the cup back under her nose and forced her to drink the rest of the liquid.

"Don't forget it," Quinn replied. Risk's eyes fluttered again, sliding closed for a moment before she opened and stared at her sister. It appeared to Quinn that she didn't want to close her eyes, as if she feared doing so would bring an end to the realization that she was no longer imprisoned and waiting for tortures to befall her. "It's alright," Quinn whispered, stroking her hair back from her face, careful of her horns. "I'll be here when you wake. Sleep now."

Risk's eyes drifted shut and Quinn waited another moment, but once it appeared that she was well and truly asleep, Quinn stood from the bed and took several steps away, meeting Lorraine halfway across the room.

"Thank you," Quinn started, but Lorraine shook her head.

"Don't thank me just yet," Lorraine said, her stare hard. "I have a lot of questions and I expect answers."

Quinn nodded. "I assumed as much."

"Does Lazarus know?"

"No."

"Who is she?"

Quinn looked back over her shoulder, taking in Risk's waif thin form on the bed. "She's my sister," Quinn finally said, turning back to take in Lorraine's shocked expression. "And she's been hurt."

Lorraine collected herself instantly, blinking and shooting glances over Quinn's shoulder. "Well, of course she's been hurt. Anyone could tell that girl's been through an ordeal. What happened?"

Quinn shook her head. "I can't go into it all right now, but she's skittish. She has a hard time being touched." Dark, festering thoughts rose from within as well as a desire—a hunger for vengeance. Taking a breath, Quinn reached out and took Lorraine's arm, steering her back toward the door as they moved even further from the bed. "I might need you again," Quinn said, keeping her voice low, "to keep watch over her. She can't be approached right now, and she most certainly can't be touched by a man. Since you're a woman, she's less volatile, but she's untrusting."

"The poor child . . ." Lorraine's gaze clouded over with tears as she raised shaking fingers to her lips. "What she must have been through. Those wounds . . ."

Quinn hadn't realized that Lorraine had seen them given Risk was already dressed when she came in the first time, but she must have glimpsed the bruises around her collarbone and left cheek at the very least. Quinn grimaced at the realization, shaking away the discomfort she felt at Lorraine's sympathy. It wasn't for her, after all, and if anyone deserved sympathy, it was Risk.

"It's not good," Quinn admitted, biting down on her urge to leave the house and go rip into the people she knew were responsible until there was nothing left of their remains but blood and decay. It took a few moments for Quinn to bring herself back to the present, and when she did, she noticed that Lorraine's attention was now focused solely on her. Quinn released her arm. "I might need you to take care of her for me for now. I might need you to help her . . . do things . . ."

"Do things?" Lorraine echoed, confused.

"She can't walk well," Quinn said. "She'll need help getting up and down. She might need help eating. She hasn't been fed well, she nearly made herself sick with just some bread and fruit earlier."

"Yes, I see." Lorraine nodded to the floor and Quinn followed her line of sight to see the fruit Risk hadn't been able to finish earlier was sitting, half-eaten, on the ground near her feet. She bent and picked it up. "You will tell Lazarus, though, won't you?" Lorraine asked.

"Yes," Quinn answered. "I will. Soon."

Lorraine inhaled and then sighed. "Alright, then," she said. "Whatever you need, I'll help. I can't begin to understand why anyone would hurt a person like this, but I will do my best to help her on her road to recovery. I assume you'll want to keep her away from the others?"

"I'd like to keep her presence here a secret," Quinn replied and then followed up with another explanation, "at least until I tell Lazarus."

Lorraine frowned, but managed a nod as she moved back toward the door, her hand lifting toward the knob. "I understand," she said. "I'll keep it to myself for now, but Quinn . . ." She lifted her gaze to meet Lorraine's. "Do not keep her a secret for too long."

"I won't," Quinn agreed. In fact, she intended to tell Lazarus as soon as Risk got some rest. She didn't know if he'd want to meet her and she doubted Risk would be able to handle Lazarus' presence at the moment, given the way she'd reacted to Lorraine.

"You're not alone," Lorraine said. "I promise you this, I will help you care for her as if she were my own daughter." Quinn felt a thanks come to her tongue once more and Lorraine must have sensed it as well, for she shook her head and retreated to the door. With one last look at Risk, Lorraine pinched her trembling lips together. "May Telerah give you both some peace this night," she said, her voice barely a whisper across the space between them. "Goodnight, Quinn."

"Goodnight," Quinn echoed as the door closed behind the other woman.

Lorraine's exit somehow left Quinn with a sense of loss, an emptiness in her chest as she turned back to the bed, taking in Risk's shape on top of the sheets. After all this time, she'd finally come back and found what she was looking for. But her objective was far from finished, she thought as she clenched her fists.

The juice of the dappa fruit dribbled from between her fingers as she stared at her sister, watching the younger girl sleep and rest for perhaps the first time in the ten years since she'd left this godsforsaken country. Ruby red droplets slipped from Quinn's fist, splattering across the wood floorboards like raining blood.

Soon. She promised herself. *Soon won't come soon enough.*

A Warning Unheeded

"Be careful of starting a war with fear, for she is patient but never kind."
— Quinn Darkova, vassal of House Fierté, fear twister, white raksasa, second daughter of the Darkova Household, vigilant murderess

The comfort of darkness clung to her as she rolled over. Quinn had just pulled the blanket up higher when the banging started. Her eyes opened, needing only a second to process the noise for what it was.

Guards.

She glanced over her shoulder. Despite the

noise, Risk slept soundly beneath two thick throws, her matted white hair splayed in clumps over the pillow. Quinn pressed her lips together and ignored the pang in her chest as she stood, rubbing the sleep from her eyes. Across the room, her reflection stared back and Quinn grimaced—thankful she'd wiped the blood from her skin before bed—even if her leathers were dirty.

Guards couldn't arrest her for dirt.

She turned for the door, taking care to ease it open as silently as possible. Quinn slipped into the hall, closing it shut behind her. When the lock clicked, she turned and bolted for the front of the house.

"What's all that bangin'?" Axe grumbled, stumbling out of her own room. She wiped the drool from her chin and patted her wild hair down, but there wasn't much the young pirate could do to tame the mess. It needed a good brush and some clippers.

"I don't know," Lazarus said, striding past Quinn. She swallowed hard and shoved all thoughts and feelings of Risk and the day before away as she masked her face in neutrality.

Lazarus grasped the handle, turning it. The lock had only just clicked when the panel was shoved open. Lazarus stepped back, brows furrowing as several guards dressed in gray and carrying spears stormed inside.

She felt his attention fly to her as the guards took station around the room. Draeven, Vaughn, and Dominicus, who'd all been sitting at the table, looked up and froze. Lorraine came walking down the hall and asked, "What's going on?" She clutched both hands to her chest and narrowed her eyes at the soldiers.

"Quinn?" Lazarus prompted.

She opened her mouth to reply, when another voice cut through the air. "Search the premises." Quinn stilled. She had to remind herself to breathe and appear nonchalant as she turned around and faced Loralye. "If you see anything or *anyone* suspicious, the Council will need to evaluate it."

Her eyebrows rose as soldiers started to break off and run down the halls. She didn't dare look toward the room she just came from, but without so much as a wave of her hand—she made it *disappear.* Invisible wisps, from Quinn's own supply of power, formed an illusion. A wall took the place of where her door was, masking it from view. Quinn hoped that the sleeping tea tonic Risk had taken the night before would keep her sedated for just a while longer.

The last thing they needed was for her to wake up and come searching, only to be found.

No, so long as she stayed put, they would never know.

"What—pray tell—is the reason for this search, dearest sister?" Quinn asked her as she and two other councillors strode into the house, along with both their parents. Ethel Darkova walked stiffly beside her husband, but it was Percinius that drew Quinn's attention. Her father's features were that of a barely contained rage.

She wondered which of her crimes they'd found out about, or if it was all of them.

"Edward is dead," Loralye spat. Her sister's fists clenched in warning, and Quinn quirked a brow.

"Dead?" she repeated. To Lazarus she said in Norcastan, "Her husband was found dead. Judging by the guards, I'm assuming they suspect us."

Lazarus cocked his head, those dark eyes cutting through her with such intensity. She suspected he wanted to ask if their suspicions were founded, but all he replied with was, "Then I suppose we should let them search."

"It's not as if we have any choice," Dominicus

said stiffly.

"They better not touch my—" Axe started up. Quinn held up a hand to quiet her as another councillor started talking.

"He was found washed up on the beach," he said. This councillor was not one Quinn was familiar with, but the Laltihr symbol pinned upon his robe identified him for her. "Weighed down by stones." Both he and Norlinda Sorvent stood there, aloof but observant.

"I see," Quinn said, brushing her thumb over her bottom lip. "Although, I must admit I'm confused why we're being searched. It sounds as if the man killed himself." She dropped her hand and raised her eyes to the ceiling. "May the gods judge his soul by his heart and not his actions."

Quinn was fairly certain his heart was blacker than hers and the death she gave him was kinder than what he deserved. She didn't mention that.

"Edward showed no signs of the darkness," Loralye said tersely. Her mouth pressed into a hard line.

"And you, a water weaver, knew the desires in his heart so well?" Quinn asked, subtly squinting at her. Loralye blanched, and Quinn wondered if she understood the double meaning behind her words.

"I am his *wife*," she spat angrily.

"Was," Quinn corrected. "Now his successor, if I do believe?" She glanced over at Norlinda Sorvent and the man of House Laltihr, raising an eyebrow. Both councillors exchanged a look and Norlinda nodded reluctantly.

"How dare you," Loralye seethed. "I'm a grieving widow—"

"And I'm merely pointing out that we're guests of the Council and you've come here with suspicions just short of blatant accusations about your late husband's death. I find it a little odd, given we have nothing to gain from this." Quinn motioned to her party, who were all silent as the grave and waiting expectantly. "But you do."

"That's preposterous—" her father started, his voice rising.

"Is it?" Quinn interrupted. "He either killed himself or was murdered, and Loralye is the only one with anything to gain from a murder. She's your heir and his wife, but hasn't bore a child. Perhaps the only way she saw fit to get power was to—"

"Quinn," Percinius barked harshly. "That's enough."

She cut her father a cold, terrible glance. "Well,

if it wasn't murder, perhaps he weighed his pockets with stones and drowned himself in the ocean." She repeated his words back to him from that first night home. "Such a tragedy."

She didn't sound sincere in the slightest, but Norlinda Sorvent nodded twice. "Perhaps the girl has a point . . ."

Loralye glared, but her mother, Ethel, began shifting side to side.

They understood the warning.

Her parents and her sister knew that she had killed him, they probably even had guesses as to why, but unless they wanted her to start revealing their nasty little secrets, they couldn't say a word that would incriminate her. She'd tied up all their options.

"By all means, councillors, please continue to search." She waved her hand flippantly to the side. "My Lord is quite understanding, and we have nothing to hide."

Minutes passed but not a single soldier found anything incriminating, nor anyone.

"Loralye . . ." the Laltihr councillor started, "perhaps your husband's death has compromised your judgement, dear girl."

Her sister turned, and gave the weathered man

a look of pure spite but the only thing she said was, "I'm fine. Thank you for your concern, Councillor."

"Yes, well," Ethel Darkova started. "Perhaps this was a hasty assumption—"

"Councillors," one of the soldiers called. "We've found something."

Quinn's heart stopped in her chest.

If they found her . . .

From the other side of the house, a man came out carrying skulls . . .

"Hey!" Axe yelled, jumping to her feet. "Those are mine." She jumped to her feet but thought better at rushing them when Vaughn followed, resting a palm on her shoulder.

"You're not to battle the white folk of the North, little pirate." He waggled his finger back and forth and Axe crossed her arms over her chest, blowing out an exaggerated breath.

Quinn glanced back to the councillors and said, "The emissary from Ilvas claims this is hers." Quinn could hardly contain her smirk when Sorvent and Laltihr both scrunched their noses in disgust.

"*What* is it?" Laltihr asked.

Quinn relayed the question and Axe said, "I like

to hunt the rats in the palace. Madara said keepin' their bodies was gross, so I skinned them and made a necklace out of their skulls."

She shook her head and told the councillors what Axe said. The guard dropped the string of skulls and Axe wiggled out of Vaughn's grip— lunging for her prize. She snatched up the rope before it hit the ground and held it close to her chest, narrowing her eyes at the guard as he hustled by.

"I'm inclined to agree with Norlinda. This was a pointless excavation." Without another word, the two councillors headed out and most of the guards trailed behind them. Loralye stood with Percinius and Ethel at her back. Her features steeped in anger.

"I know you did it," she hissed. Her normally beautiful features contorted by rage and grief. She may have truly loved her monster of a husband.

Quinn leaned forward and whispered, "I warned you not to start a war with me. You should have listened while you still had the chance."

She kissed her sister on the cheek, blowing a breath of black magic into her skin. Loralye trembled and hugged her arms closer. Whatever anger she felt was quickly fizzling out as fear took precedence.

Quinn stepped away and Ethel grabbed her eldest daughter and pulled her close as if she were a mere babe.

"This isn't over," Percinius said.

He strode out the front door, leaving his wife and daughter to follow. The rest of the guards exited, and Quinn stood on the porch until they were out of sight. She pivoted and walked back in, closing the front door firmly.

"Would you care to tell me why the inquisition came down on us?" Lazarus started. He pointed to the side and up, directly where Quinn's room should have been. "And why there is a girl in there that you hid?"

Quinn sighed. "I suppose I might have some explaining to do."

Lazarus' eyes flashed as he kicked a chair out from the table. He took a seat, resting his elbows on his knees. His fingers steepled together, but there was no mistaking the barely contained flame that burned beneath his skin.

"Start talking."

Whatever It Takes

"There is no such thing as a tame animal. All of us are wild, but some choose to submit when a stronger alpha comes about—for the lure of power can be too great, even for animals."

— *Quinn Darkova, vassal of House Fierté, fear twister, white raksasa, second daughter of the Darkova Household, devious murderess*

Silence.

It stretched between them as Lazarus looked at Quinn, and she stared back resolutely.

"Allow me to get this correct," Lazarus said, his words clipped and stern as he spoke for the first time since Quinn had finished her explanations. "You tortured and killed your sister's husband. Used the information you gleaned from him to find and rescue a prisoner and brought her back here, thus bringing down the whole of the N'skari Council and their scrutiny upon us." He paused, lifting his brows. "Is that all?"

Quinn nodded. "That sufficiently sums it up, yes."

"I see." Lazarus took a step away, pivoting and facing the room as he paced the length of it and then turned, striding back.

Quinn regarded him as he moved, sensing his rising emotions even though not a glimmer cracked through the mask he wore—she couldn't tell which was winning out. He stopped before her once more, but instead of looking at her, he faced Draeven.

"Give us a moment alone." It wasn't a question. Draeven nodded, and as a unit the rest of them— Dominicus, Draeven, and Lorraine—began to file out. Vaughn, confused, but nonetheless use to following commands, went after Draeven. Axe, on the other hand, remained right where she was, staring openly at Lazarus and Quinn with a combination of excitement and intrigue.

"Come on, little pirate," Vaughn said with a

huff, picking up the girl around her middle and carting her away. "We leave now."

A squawk of outrage followed as she slapped his hand, nearly letting the grotesque necklace of rat skulls slip from her grip. "Unhand me, ya big, overfed brute!" she yelled. "I want to know what's gonna happen." Her cries and sounds of frustration tapered off as Vaughn carried her up the stairs and out of hearing distance.

"You try my patience, Quinn," Lazarus said.

"It had to be done," she replied with no hint of remorse. She had killed and had plans to kill more before her objective was seen through.

"I'm gathering that," Lazarus said, leveling her with a dark look that she met and held. "We have much to discuss."

Quinn nodded. "Ask your questions."

"Will I get an answer this time?" Lazarus shot back.

"Yes."

The answer was sharp. A promise. An oath to him. Quinn had accepted that her timeline had moved up when she'd killed Edward, she'd courted the clock when she took Risk. In some ways she was surprised she'd been able to hold Lazarus at bay this long, but it was time to bring him in.

She'd need him, after all, if she wanted to pull it all off.

"What does this mean for the alliance?" he asked.

Quinn shook her head and strode around him as her belly gurgled in hunger. Lazarus followed her to the kitchen where she picked up a dappa fruit from the bowl on the wooden table in the center of the room. She bit into the outer layer of skin, chewed and swallowed the tangy flesh before answering.

"I haven't forgotten my promise," she assured him. "You will have your alliance, but it won't be like it was in Ilvas, or even how it was with the Ciseans."

Lazarus folded his arms across his massive chest and narrowed his eyes. "What do you mean?" he demanded.

Quinn scowled. "You were a fool to think you could sail into N'skari waters with no repercussions. If it wasn't for me, everyone on your ship would've been dead before you reached the shores. The N'skari do not give alliances, as I'm sure you've figured out by now." She bit viciously into the fruit in her hand, chewing as she glared at him.

Lazarus' gaze was a roaring fire. She courted

danger when she played games with him, but couldn't find it in her to stop or look away. He took a step toward her, letting his hands fall to his sides. Another step followed and then another, until her back pressed against the edge of the table. "I've allowed you much freedom, Quinn." When he spoke, it was with a rasping darkness. A layer of warning that sent a spike of alertness up her spine. "You call me a fool and I've let you, but do you really think I would have walked into a dangerous situation without some sort of backup? Without a plan? Do you honestly believe I would've been struck down by the N'skari Maji? With their sticks and spears and insignificant little beliefs?"

Burning hot coals in his eyes drifted down as his breath touched her face. Against her pale white skin, his tanned flesh was made even more prominent. Quinn swallowed the last of her bite. Dropping the remainder of the fruit on the table's surface, she tilted her chin up and glared at him.

"If you want your alliance, the only way to get it is subjugation." He leaned away, but didn't say anything. She took that as her cue to keep going. "You need to have complete control of the Council if you want to make sure they don't renege on whatever agreements you have set up."

"And for you?" he asked, one eyebrow lifting. "What is it that you want, Quinn? What is your reason for playing games this time?"

Quinn didn't hesitate to answer.

"I want Loralye and my parents dead."

He nodded, seeming unsurprised. Quinn wondered how he was able to keep such an impassive face, but then realized that Lazarus wasn't like normal men. By Mazzulah, he wasn't much of a human man at all. He was far darker, vicious—a savage in civilized clothing.

"And just how long have you been planning this?" he asked.

"For ten years." Ever since she'd been chained to a line of strange men and women; led onto a ship bound for the southern nations as a man handed over a purse of coins to her parents. Her father had beaten her, and her mother stood aside, watching as she was carried away without a single tear.

Or perhaps longer, she briefly thought. *At least for Loralye.* Maybe it started the first time her elder sister used her abilities to make Quinn's blood sing and burn in her veins.

How or when it had begun wasn't important. It was now the end that Quinn was focused on.

"Alright, then." Lazarus had moved a step as Quinn had been contemplating her thoughts and she was free to relax now, reaching once more to the fruit. She took a moment to peel the rest of the skin away—though it could be eaten, the fruit in her hand was not as fresh, and the exterior was harder and less sweet than she preferred. Tossing the skin away, she finished consuming the dappa as Lazarus spoke again. "What is your next step?" he asked. "Who's next on your list?"

"Loralye."

He frowned as if truly surprised by that, but instead of asking for a reason, he merely nodded and asked, "When?"

"Tomorrow," Quinn replied with a grin as the details came together in her mind.

"And until then?" he prompted.

"Until then, I need to prepare."

"How will you kill her?" he asked, curious.

Quinn would have liked to say slowly, painfully, brutally, or any combination therein. But instead, she had other plans. Something far more devious, something even her parents wouldn't see coming no matter how well they thought they knew the twisted child she had once been. She was no longer a child, but a woman. A woman full of even more ruthless intention than they remembered.

"Carefully," Quinn finally answered. "Very carefully." She lifted her gaze to meet his. "And I'll need your help to do it."

Lazarus didn't balk at the suggestion. He simply nodded and said, "Just tell me what you need, and we'll have it done. So long as you ensure my alliance by the end, you can take who or what you need, Quinn. I will have my victory and you'll have yours. Whatever it takes."

"Whatever it takes," she agreed.

Bad Memories and Brighter Days

"To take a person's choice from them is to take their freedom."
— Quinn Darkova, vassal of House Fierté, fear twister,
white raksasa, second daughter of the Darkova Household,
expectant murderess

Quinn closed the door behind her. The lock clicked softly, and she let out a sigh, glancing toward the bed. Risk sat there, huddled in the corner. She stared at Quinn with wide eyes as she clutched the blankets to her chest.

It was obvious Risk had been awoken by the guards. Quinn was only thankful she hadn't come out of the room, but that still left her unsure of what to say that would make this easier. What words could dissuade her sister's fears? She took a step for the bed and said, "Risk, I—"

"Left me." Risk didn't sound angry. Only resigned. That broke Quinn's heart how easily her little sister lost faith, but how could she help her? How could she make her understand what had happened?

She didn't know, but she had to try.

"Only for a little while," she said, slowly moving toward the bed. She lowered herself onto the edge and leaned forward, resting her head in her hands.

"But you're going to again," Risk said. Quinn didn't try to deny it.

"Yes, I will again, but I'll come back again too." She lowered her hands to the bed and fisted them in the sheets as she looked back over her shoulder. "You know that, right? That I'll come back?"

Risk's lips pinched together, and she lowered her haunting, damnable eyes. "I used to think that," she whispered. "In the beginning, when Lady Darkova and Lady Loralye escorted me away. They brought me to the temple and had me clean myself. They said I was dirty. That what came next, I brought it on myself." Her sister's hands shook, her knuckles near white. Quinn swallowed, hating the words that spilled out of her mouth, but she knew she needed to hear them and listen. Listen as no one probably had or possibly ever would again. "They put me on an altar that night, and every time they . . ." she paused, sucking in a harsh breath. "I thought of you. I thought you would come for me. They said you were gone and never coming back, and I didn't believe them. Until, one day, I did."

Quinn turned, pulling her leg up onto the bed so she could look at Risk more fully. She wanted to apologize and tell her she was sorry for not being there, but the fact of it was she never could have been. That choice, along with so many others, had been ripped from her grasp.

Quinn decided to tell her something else, something she never told anyone.

"They said the same thing to me when they sold me. Except instead of dirty, I was simply evil. Twisted. They told me that I brought it on myself and that if the gods of light couldn't correct me, nor could my father's firm hand, perhaps the slave-masters of the south could." Quinn's voice leveled out, apathetic dispassion filling her as she skirted over the dregs of her past—a past that had tormented her for too long. She wasn't a slave anymore. She wasn't a victim, but those scars still marred her flesh and the ones on her skin weren't near as deep as the others—the ones no one could see. "The journey south took a month. They kept us under the deck, stored like animals, chained together by the wrists and ankles. I can still feel the stifling heat and smell the stench of piss and death." Quinn had to suppress a shudder as it started at the top of her spine and ran through her. "When we finally got to the port, I thought the worst of it was over. Surely nothing could be as terrible as the journey . . . and I was wrong." Flashes of bare skin crowding her swam before her eyes. She felt the heat of the sun, harsh in the winters but unbearable in the summers. Ghost manacles rubbed her wrists raw, and the clench of hunger in her stomach still plagued her. Above all, it was the crack of a whip that had a jolt running through her body.

Quinn tensed, breathing hard as she pushed the memories back to the corners of her mind that were too dark—

"It wasn't your fault," Risk whispered.

"I know," Quinn replied, though her jaw clenched. "It wasn't yours either."

At that, her sister shook her head. "But I'm—"

"Tainted?" Quinn said. Risk pressed her lips together but nodded. "All that means is our mother fucked a raksasa and you were born. Who your father was doesn't change who or what you are. That's for you and only you to decide."

"I have a demon's blood," she said. Not outwardly arguing but still clinging to false ideals from religious bigots.

"And I'm a fear twister," Quinn told her. "My magic chose me, and it's one of the darkest magics there is. Does that mean I deserved what I got?" she asked her.

"No, of course not—"

"Then neither did you." Risk fell silent and regarded her cautiously. "You don't get to choose your blood, but the men who locked you up and did those things to you." She paused as Risk started to shut down. "They claimed to follow the gods of light, but I haven't heard of a light god doing that to anyone. Not even a raksasa." *For all N'skara's stories, the raksasa were created by the gods—the same as humanity. Who were they to judge what was good or evil?*

Quinn found herself asking that question again and again the longer she lived.

"I hate them," Risk whispered.

"Good," Quinn said. Her sister blinked, her eyebrows drawing together. "Hold onto that hate. You're going to need it when this is all over."

Risk started to frown. "What do you mean?"

"I'm going to take care of the monsters in N'skara. I'll show them what a real one looks like, and when I'm done—we're going to leave." Quinn pulled both legs up and crossed them at the ankles. "When days get hard and long, you'll need that fire —that hate—to remind you where you were so that you become strong enough to never be there again."

In a small voice, Risk asked, "Will it ever get better?"

"It will," Quinn nodded. "I know you can't see that just yet, but I promise better days are coming. I just have to finish business here, and for that, I will have to leave again." They'd come full circle, and in that time, Risk had slowly inched forward, bringing her knees up to her chest and wrapping her arms around them. It was the same pose she'd had when Quinn had found her in the temple. Her chest clenched as the girl lowered her head and rested her chin on the tops of her knees.

"I'm worried they'll take you again," she said. "I'm worried they'll hurt you too."

Quinn let out a short, barking laugh. "I'd love to see them try." She grinned wickedly, but Risk didn't look amused.

"I'm serious," Risk said, her sad blue eyes pulling Quinn back to their grim reality.

She leaned forward and rested her hand on the sheet before Risk, palm up. A silent offer. Risk took it, extending a delicate hand the color of rain-filled skies to grab hers tightly.

"Nothing bad is going to happen to me," Quinn told her, gripping as tight as she could without hurting her. "But I do need to ask . . . when I carry out my revenge, is there anyone that you want to see to yourself?"

She remained still, noting the way Risk gave away nothing as she asked, "You mean kill?"

"Yes," Quinn said. "I mean kill."

Risk seemed to consider that for a long time as they sat there. Then she said, "Does it make me a coward if I tell you no?"

"I don't think so."

"And if I said yes?" Risk asked. "Would that make me strong? Would it take the pain away?"

"I . . ." Quinn struggled for words. "I don't know what to say."

Risk nodded, as if she expected that answer. "I'm not strong enough to kill anyone myself. You and I both know that. I would just slow you down and possibly get you hurt . . ." Quinn could hear the hesitation. The inquiry. "Out of all my abusers, there are only two that I want to see end, even if I'm not the one to do it."

"Who?" Quinn asked.

"Our mother, for having me," Risk said. There was no pity, no sympathy, or sorrow in her voice. "Lord Darkova for being the first and the worst of the men that took from me." A roaring filled her ears. Quinn's heartbeat pounded so loud she barely heard Risk's next words. "If I can see them die, I think I'll finally be able to sleep knowing the world is a better place. Even with someone like me in it."

"I'll make it happen," Quinn said. "You'll be there."

Risk nodded, but didn't say anything, falling deep inside herself. Quinn worried about that. Worried about leaving her alone. "You know, to set this in place, I'll need to leave for a time. I worry about you being in here alone, though. Would you be open to Lorraine possibly—"

"No," Risk shook her head and snatched her hand away.

Quinn sighed. She knew it would be this way, but she hoped. "You didn't even hear the rest of what I was saying."

"You want your friend to watch over me," Risk

said. Her expression turned hostile. Guarded. *Perhaps that wasn't the greatest way to broach the subject*, she admitted to herself. Reminding her of a past abuser and then asking to leave her in someone's care probably wasn't the best way to go about it.

"I don't know her, and I don't trust her. If you want me to stay here, then *no one* guards me." She didn't twitch, even though fear began fuming from her skin. Plumes of black smoke drifted over the bed, drawn to Quinn. She cast it away, trying to calm her sister, but nothing short of an agreement was going to do it.

"I need someone to be with you in case you need anything, not guard you." Quinn said. *And in case they send anyone here when I'm away.*

She wasn't going to tell her sister that, though, not when the mere thought of a person terrified her. Let alone someone from N'skara.

"I can take care of myself," Risk said. Neither of them believed that to be true, but she was unmoving, and Quinn understood why. Risk was untrusting of all persons and their intentions. While she had been a kind and considerate child—fate was cruel, and she wasn't so lucky to be able to grow into such a woman. While she tolerated Lorraine's presence temporarily, it was a means to an end. Quinn pondered that for a moment, when an idea struck her.

Risk was not only part raksasa, but a beast tamer. Her magic lay in communicating and sometimes even controlling the animals around her. It was the only place in this world she held a modicum of control, and Quinn wondered if perhaps it might be the way.

"What if the thing watching wasn't a person?" she asked.

Risk frowned and tilted her head. One of her horns stabbed at the blanket draped around her, not that she seemed to notice. "What do you mean?"

Quinn turned her hand back over and whispered, "Neiss, come forward."

The mauve snake slithered up her spine and over her shoulder. It wound its way down her arm, moving forward until it peeked out of her cuff. His slender head slid out as he separated from her skin and became whole. Slowly he parted from her flesh, taking on a tangible skin of his own.

Risk gasped and the serpent froze.

Her arms unfolded and her knees dropped as she leaned forward, extending a tentative hand. "Is that a basilisk?" her sister breathed. Neiss looked to

Quinn who nodded, and then slowly rose to brush over Risk's fingers.

"It is. I call him Neiss," Quinn answered as the snake took a liking toward her. The dark gray of her lips turned up as he slithered closer, running over her exposed legs.

"How did he end up inside you?" she asked, her eyes glowed brighter for a brief moment.

"It's a long story," Quinn said, "but he might be able to tell you?" She mentally nudged the snake, who was contentedly settling himself around Risk.

"He can," her sister said after a pause. "He's not like other animals, but I'm still able to talk to him." She turned her hand and brushed the back of it over his purple scales.

"Would this be an acceptable compromise?" Quinn asked her. "Would you find his company agreeable when I need to be gone?"

Risk thought for a moment as Neiss coiled up on her lap and then settled in as if to sleep. A faint smile ghosted her lips.

"Yes," she nodded. "I would."

Cold Fire Burning

"Feed the flames and soon enough you become the fire."
— Lazarus Fierté, soul eater, heir to Norcasta, morally
ambiguous warlord

Hatred was fuel to the world. So little did people realize it, how many of them were led by hate. They let it consume them and drive them to do unspeakable things, often without their knowledge. Lazarus saw it now in Quinn. The difference was that she knew the emotions that drove her, and she accepted their darkness willingly.

She herded Axe through the barren streets of Liph, the smaller girl concealed under a dark cloak.

Quinn kept her focus forward, her arm slung almost protectively over Axe . . . as she would were the girl someone else, someone he had yet to meet face-to-face. According to Quinn, her younger sister was volatile, particularly against men.

He could easily understand why, from what he'd been told both by her and Lorraine.

A burn swept under his skin as he silently slid from his hiding place down a narrow alley and followed the two figures he'd been trailing since they left their accommodations. Quinn believed that her elder sister, the Lady Loralye, would be expecting something like this. He suspected she was right. Loralye hadn't left their accommodations willingly yesterday. Had she been able to search the premises they had resided in by tearing it apart brick by brick, she would have. It was clear the woman was not exactly thinking in the right of mind, especially if she thought she could win against Quinn.

No. *Saevyana* was carried by her hatred and bloodlust this night and he doubted anyone aside from himself could handle her when she was in such a mood. Her determination was a burning fire that drew him like a moth to flame—or perhaps the air was a better comparison. Moths went, but did not understand the burn—but the wind fanned the flame and they both grew strong as a result. This night Lazarus was that bitter cold to her flame.

Bright they would burn. Together.

Lazarus moved through the streets, following at a careful distance from the two shadows in front of him. He was transfixed by Quinn's movements, yet wondered still if she had underestimated her elder sister's intelligence. She had left her own cloak off— no doubt in preparation for a fight—and her lavender hair shined silver under the moonlight.

He tipped his own face up and considered the clear skies. Strange that the clouds would disperse on this night when a low hanging air of rain and snow had hung over the city since they'd arrived. He almost believed that the gods might have been aiding them.

Lazarus reached the building Quinn and her charge had rounded just moments before and paused as the sounds of a scuffle reached his ears. Putting on a burst of speed, he darted forward, only to come up short.

Quinn had been right.

Lady Loralye had come. Her face was a pale glowing moon in the darkness as her scowl turned on her sister. Quinn stood tall and proud, a hardness in her expression, a small, wicked grin upon her lips. One of the men to Lady Loralye's right ripped away the cloak that covered Axe.

The red-haired little girl raised a hand and waved. "Hi there," she said. None of the men, nor Loralye, could understand the Norcastan words, but the gesture served its purpose.

Lady Loralye turned accusing eyes on Quinn. "Das en vana?" Lazarus didn't have to know N'skaran to understand what she was asking. She had expected another underneath the disguise and was outraged to find that she had been duped.

Quinn tossed her head back, the echo of her laughter so loud and long that after a while, it made the soldiers at Loralye's back shift with a wary confusion. They knew a dangerous creature when they saw one. Mere guards with only the brute strength of their hands, the fools had no clue of the beast they had unleashed. Their eyes turned collectively to their master, and Lady Loralye pointed a long elegant finger, sending the lot of them to their deaths with a sharp barking command.

Lazarus felt a growl rise up within his chest as they nodded and converged. The clash of metal meeting metal reached his ears and he realized that Axe had already moved to block the first of the raining blows. Wide eyes flashing and hair swishing at her back, she whirled around and brought the blade of one of her axes across the throat of her attacker. Blood poured and the man dropped his weapon to clutch at his open throat.

Quinn said something he couldn't understand, stepping to the side as one of the soldiers barreled toward her. Her laughter had fallen away in the face of battle, but there was no denying the enjoyment she took in killing.

She didn't hesitate to send a burst of her power, black smoking wisps pouring from her hands. When it reached the ground, the magic dispersed, scattering into small, bug-like beings that encroached upon the soldier and sent him into a fit of madness as they crawled up his body, into his mouth, nostrils, eyes, and ears. His screams were abruptly cut off a moment later and the darkness that had encompassed him receded, revealing the face of the soldier—white with death and stretched in agony and horror.

Quinn was holding nothing back this night.

"Aye," Axe called out as she was besieged by more soldiers, despite what they had witnessed of their companion. "I could use a little help over here!"

Biting back a curse, Lazarus withdrew the

sword at his hip and bolted forward. He disrupted the downward swing of a spear, jerking his arm upward and sending the boy wielding it stumbling back. Exhaling heavily in annoyance, he made quick work of the guard, slicing first across his abdomen. The boy paused and looked up at him in abject fear and confusion—as if he couldn't yet feel the pain of his own death. Lazarus was merciful as he brought his blade back down once more, severing the boy's head before the pain could truly reach him.

That boy was lucky as the next attacker did not receive the same treatment. Lazarus lopped off the hand that reached for him and the offending limb dropped to the ground with a thud. The dagger in his free hand slipped from his fingers as he stumbled back, waving the bloody stump about. Lazarus paused as a whistle slid past his ear and an axe imbedded itself in the man's forehead, halting all sound.

Pivoting and glancing over his shoulder, Lazarus saw Axe lift her hand and the slight squelch of the weapon leaving the soldier's skull on its own accord was a sound he'd never forget as it came flying back to her. She looked at him and grinned. "What?" she asked. "He was annoyin' me." She turned back to her next foe.

Just as well, Lazarus thought. They needed to finish the guards or they'd risk being discovered before Quinn was finished.

The remaining battle was as swift as it was quiet. The soldiers following Quinn's sister Loralye knew the extent of their treachery. They kept their voices low except in the instances just before their deaths, to which he and Axe quickly dispatched them before they could draw unwanted notice.

The two worked in tandem, making their way through the swaths of gray robes. It couldn't have been more than a few minutes before no more remained. By the end, Axe panted as if she'd run several miles. She fell backwards, her hair landing in a pool of blood, not that the girl seemed to care.

"That was fun, but I'm tired now." She let out a groan before lifting her head to look at him. "Do we have anythin' to eat?"

Lazarus shook his head and leaned down to clean his blade on the robe of a dead man. The corpse didn't twitch and he sheathed the blade once it shined silver once more.

Bodies were strewn about, blood soaking in between the crevices of each stone. Lazarus turned, seeking out Quinn. She hadn't been in the middle of the fight. *Where had she gone?*

He spotted her several paces away, but it was only when Lazarus pulled his attention from her that he saw her sister, Lady Loralye, had fallen to her knees.

Lazarus edged closer, moving to see what Quinn was doing.

A lock of lavender hair lifted against the wind as she whispered something low to her sister, causing the other woman to sob and clutch at her chest. A haze of black wisps poured from Quinn—from her fingertips, her hair, her very being—so much of it flowed that if Lazarus had not known what she was, it would have looked to him as though she were on fire. The smoke-like tendrils circled and clung to Lady Loralye, sliding into every visible orifice. It streamed from her eyes as she sobbed, curled into her ears even as she cupped her hands over the sides of her head to ward it off, and gushed from between her lips like the plague.

Her sobs carried on the wind as she rocked back and forth. Her eyes unfocused. Loralye scratched at her head and pounded against her skull with the palms of her hands. She'd had to have been doing this for several minutes now, for there were long, deep scratches already forming on her neck and cheeks. She dug her nails into her skin, trying—hard as she might—to rid herself of the power pouring into her.

Quinn took a single step forward and knelt at the woman's side. She whispered something in her elder sister's ear and whatever it was made the woman jerk and begin wailing; fear and pain twisting in a cruel symphony as the power of her cries rose into the air.

"Uhhh, Lazarus?" Axe approached from behind. "I think we gotta go."

Lazarus pulled his gaze from Quinn's scene of vengeance. As drunk as he was on the sight, he knew the child was right. Voices in the distance warned him that they were nearly out of time.

Whirling back to Quinn, he saw that she'd stood and was making her way toward him as Loralye tried to crawl away. Black tendrils leaked from her face and ears as she scrambled back to get as far from the source of her terror as possible. She wasn't in her mind, though, as she stumbled over a severed limb and slipped on the bloodstained ground. Her white robes bled crimson instantly. How curious it was to see something so pristine soiled so quickly.

Loralye clambered back using her elbows and

arms as she bumped into one of the soldier's bodies. She turned, reaching for the dagger in his belt before swinging back to Quinn—who watched the mad woman with a detached amusement. She took a single step forward to taunt her sister. Loralye screamed, dropping the dagger and reaching for something more substantial. A fallen sword. She brandished it awkwardly as though she'd never lifted something as heavy as a sword's weight before.

"We need to go," Lazarus said, directing the words to Quinn.

She nodded, but kept her attention centered squarely on her sister.

"Are we just gonna leave this lady here?" Axe asked, scratching her head.

"Yes," Quinn replied. "Let her stay in the filth of her crimes for a little while longer. She'll be dead soon enough."

It didn't seem as though Loralye could understand them, no matter the language they had been using. Her head swung wildly about, her focus no longer on Quinn but on the air around her as though she were ready to battle—or at least attempt to ward off—invisible fiends.

"Her mind is broken," Lazarus said.

Quinn chuckled, turning to go as he took her arm. She didn't shrug him off as she normally might have. "Not quite yet, but it will be," she replied as he urged her forward. Axe trailed behind.

Lazarus took a glance down at Quinn and noticed the way the moon reflected in the depths of her crystalline irises. A cold fire still raged from within her. He wondered, as they disappeared into the shadows, if there would ever come a time when that fire of hers would die out—if that rage and aggression and even the hint of madness would ever settle.

And he hoped—though he was loath to admit it —that it never would.

Quinn was a creature unlike any other.

She was *saevyana*.

Old Souls and Older Stories

"Every story holds at least a kernel of truth."
— *Mariska Darkova*

Hold onto that hate. You're going to need it when this is all over . . .

Quinn's words echoed in her mind long after her sister had gone. They circled like buzzards, waiting for her to succumb to the yawning cavern of her hatred. Something like that would drag her down into the depths of despair. It wouldn't let her leave the prison Quinn had risked her life to save her from. Giving into her animosity so early—without planning and intention—would make her no more intelligent than a wild animal. And though beasts could be perceptive in their own ways, they were rarely rational. Often thinking of nothing more than survival. They were reactionary. Quinn had all but assured Risk that she would get her revenge. All she had to do was wait. Even if the wait would slowly drive her to the brink of madness.

It was hard not to give in. Vengeance was something she didn't just want, but craved. It was a hunger so great that it couldn't be denied. While her mind was ready and willing, her body was not. In that, she would have to cave to Quinn's wishes. Even if she wanted to do anything, she couldn't. She was far too powerless at the moment.

Pushing those thoughts away, Risk returned her attention to the basilisk her sister had left behind. Through narrow black slits outlined in yellow, the creature regarded her with a cold impenetrable gaze. Against her lap, the lower portion of its body curled tight against her and despite its small size, she could feel that it was rather heavy. For an eternity, it seemed, they stared at one another. A feeble, horned half-raksasa and a beautiful basilisk with a shimmering coat of mauve-tinted scales. The same shade as Quinn's hair, Risk noted. When last she had glimpsed Quinn, many years ago, her hair had been the same silver shade as her own, but now . . . no longer did it retain the color of moonlight. Instead, it reflected this animal's own color.

This was Quinn's compromise. Risk continued to examine the animal. There was something overtly special about it. Even if she disregarded the very fact that this creature had slid from somewhere beneath Quinn's skin, the animal itself was a strange hue. One she had never before seen on an animal and she had seen plenty of snakes that had managed to slither their way into the temple prison she had been held in—along with all manner of other beasts.

"How did my sister come across you?" she finally asked the creature—Neiss, Quinn had called him.

"*She did not come across me. I was called to her from my previous master,*" the basilisk replied.

Risk's lips pinched and she pressed her aching back against the headboard as she stared down at Neiss. "Who was your previous master?"

"*The dark one.*" Risk delayed her response. Surely he would offer more in the way of information, but he didn't.

This creature was as vague as the bird that had

visited her in her cell. There was no possible way for Risk to know who this 'dark one' that he spoke of was. Perhaps another friend of Quinn's. It was difficult for Risk to think of her sister having friends, though she couldn't neglect the truth that it appeared Quinn was not alone in her return to N'skara. She was not the type to trust, and seeing her do so unnerved Risk.

Vision dimming as fatigue assaulted her, Risk panted softly with the effort she exerted trying to keep her back stiff and straight and her body upright on the bed. She tired so easily, and she hated herself for it. Despised the fragile cocoon her body had become. "*There is no need to worry.*" Risk blinked and then fixed the creature with a stare.

"What do you mean?" she asked, frowning slightly.

"*Mistress will return and all will be well. Her strength is unmatched by all except the dark one.*"

"Who is this dark one you speak of?" she finally asked, leaning forward. Her hand brushed against his scales and the creature rippled against her, pressing more firmly against her grip.

"*He is the one born of souls.*"

Risk gave up, too tired to try and figure out what the animal meant. She drew her hand away with a huff as she twisted onto her side, displacing the basilisk along the top of her thighs. Closing her eyes, she hoped sleep would come. A rest before Quinn returned would make the time pass more quickly.

Something bumped against her hand again. *"You wish to speak?"* Neiss asked, squirming his body beneath her limp hand as though he desired the feel of her skin on his.

Absently, she stroked her fingers along his long slender body, marveling at the ripple in his scales. A black tongue darted out from his mouth and licked at the air. "You don't seem in the mood to talk to me," she commented. "I don't have the wherewithal to decipher your ambiguous words. Why can't you speak plainly? Why can't you simply talk to me and let me listen?"

"I don't understand." Black and yellow slits scanned her tired face. It seemed to her that he was trying, but this creature was an animal after all. Risk got the feeling that it hadn't intended to be difficult; he simply thought differently than humans did. She needed to think of a question that would give him more direction.

Letting her skin slide against the snake's body in

soft, lazy movements, she tried again. "How old are you?" she asked.

"*I am very old*," Neiss responded.

"Older than any human?"

"*Far older. I have existed since before humans were gifted with the power that flows through my mistress' veins, the same power in yours.*"

Her hand stopped, hovering over the creature. "You're older than the creation of Maji?" Risk couldn't believe it. Maji had been around for as long as humans could recall. Even she knew that. Risk stared down at the creature in her arms with a renewed sense of curiosity. Neiss bumped her with his head, nudging her into continuing her stroking. She couldn't explain why, but it wasn't unnatural for her to hold the snake closer—a creature that many feared. She felt no alarm, no creeping sensation of uneasiness, though she knew that many would.

"How much older are you?"

"*My first master, the one I will return to, gave me life. I am his first creation. A child of his flesh.*"

"What?"

"*You have stopped your touches.*"

Startled, unaware that she had been shocked to a stop once more, Risk put her palm down against his body, but this time, she did not continue her stroking. Her hand rested against him and while it seemed he liked the feel of her caresses, he did not speak again. This could be no ordinary basilisk if what he said was true. Risk felt a sensation where her skin met his scales. A low hum that resonated, as if the animal were constantly vibrating, unintentionally shivering its body at a frequency indiscernible to the naked eye.

Curious, Risk resumed her strokes as she formed her next question. "*Where* were you born?" she asked.

"*A realm far beyond this one.*"

"The Dark Realm?" Risk couldn't keep the quiver from her words. Once, she'd been resigned to go into that oblivion, but no longer. The very idea scared her. She wasn't ready now. Quinn had promised she would come back and together, they would have their vengeance.

A scaled head shook. "*I am from the first realm. It existed before the Dark or the Gray Realm.*"

There was no third realm that Risk knew of. The only other realm that he could possibly mean was that of the gods. Risk examined the basilisk with a sharper focus but there was nothing on its body, no telltale sign in its scales as it moved closer to her and allowed her to pet it. "If you were created before Maji," she said quietly, "were there others created with you?"

"*Yes. I have had many brothers and sisters.*"

"Are they here, in the human realm?" she pressed. The memory of glowing globes of honey peering at her from the shadows fluttered through her mind. "Was there a bird? Black as night and—"

"*Many creatures that inhabit this realm were created elsewhere and brought here to serve, just as I was,*" Neiss answered, cutting her off.

A crease formed between her brows. "To serve? Is that what you did before Quinn? Serve the dark one? How did you come to be with him before?"

"*I was called to his power, just as I have been to every master before. But instead of serving, I was swallowed. There was no escape until I was called forth once more to protect, and my soul was taken again, by a magic far more . . . familiar.*"

"Familiar?" Risk repeated the word. "What does that mean?"

"*Fear calls to fear.*"

Risk pressed her lips together, unsatisfied with that answer but something niggled at the back of her mind as Neiss closed his slitted gaze and settled more firmly against her side. A recollection surfaced in her mind and Risk let her eyelids slide shut as she reached out, grasping for the sliver of memory. There had once been a book in the Darkova family library that told about the gods. All N'skari books centered on the gods of light, but this one had been so old, it had likely been overlooked. Forgotten and neglected like herself. Inside this book was a story:

There was once a god of great beauty. So marvelous was his skin, so unique were his features, he was adored by all of his fellow gods. However, as eons stretched, the adoration waned and instead, the other gods grew fearful of the man's beauty. Until collectively they decided to rid him of his allure and cursed him with a head of serpents. But instead of wailing and bemoaning his misfortune, the God of Beauty instead plucked the brightest colored snake from his head and gifted it with the ability of thought. So shocked were the other gods at the man's lack of temper that they cowered from him and renamed him the God of Fear.

Risk let her gaze drop to the basilisk. *How apt,* she thought, *that Quinn had named this creature for that god.*

The God of Beauty had become the God of Fear and all because he had not feared serpents. Just as she didn't fear the basilisk.

In the Light of Day

"The truth will always find its way to the light. Why not accept it? No matter the darkness it holds."
— Quinn Darkova, vassal of House Fierté, fear twister, white raksasa, second daughter of the Darkova Household, sly murderess

A s the sun began to rise in the eastern sky, Quinn and Lazarus stepped out onto the front porch of the home they'd been living in for nine of the ten days they'd been permitted. It might have been suspect if they were found to be waiting for what they both knew was coming, but not so much when they had heard the march of soldiers in the street beforehand.

The Council guards approached, sending the few lower born citizens milling about in the street skittering into alleyways. Some turned to survey what was about to happen, but most had the good sense to not look back.

"Quinn Darkova, second heir to the Darkova House, and Lazarus Fierté of Norcasta," a man in the lightest of grays spoke. His clothing gave him authority over the other men behind him. "You are to come before the council for questioning."

Quinn didn't spare Lazarus a glance, though she could feel the sizzle of his gaze on her back. She stepped away from the curb of the street and gestured to the N'skari. "Lead the way then."

The soldier nodded and turned. Lazarus and Quinn fell into step as the rest of the battalion congregated around them. They were herded through the streets of Liph until they reached the Council's temple, watched over by the god Ramiel and the goddess Skadi. Quinn noted their pristine statues with mild distaste as they ascended the steps and she lifted her face to the sky. While just hours before, it had been cloud-less, now it was a heavy gray. Quinn grinned and tilted her face back down as she stepped through the archway into the chancel of the temple.

The dull roar of people talking in tandem and shouting over one another in the main council room wasn't shocking, but it was entertaining, as more councillors realized their presence. The yelling petered out into silence.

Ethel and Percinius Darkova stood together at their pedestal, glaring down with a hatred so strong, it marked their faces with stress lines. Quinn smiled up at them before turning her attention to Elder Emsworth as he spoke.

"Quinn Darkova, do you know why you've been called here today?"

Quinn knew exactly why she'd been called to the Council. Loralye had been found and her parents knew exactly what had happened. Quinn had sought her retribution as she had promised she would and now they were on the edge of throwing caution to the wind. They wanted to see her destroyed for her actions, but they had no proof, no motive, and most importantly—no ground to stand on.

In answer to the elder's question, Quinn lifted one shoulder. "Is it, perhaps, to discuss a true alliance between the future king of Norcasta and N'skara?" she inquired.

Upon her pedestal, Ethel Darkova sneered. "You know that's not why you're here, you heathen," she snapped. "You've done something to Loralye. Don't deny it!"

Quinn pivoted and faced her mother, leveling the older woman with a look so intense, she shriveled back against her husband. "I'm sure I don't know what you mean, *Mother*."

Elder Emsworth sighed, sounding tired as he lifted his hand, staying Percinius as he stepped up to reply. Percinius looked like he would rather take a dagger to the heart than stay his tongue, but Quinn's father merely scowled as he submitted to the elder's gesture of silence.

"Your sister, the first heir of House Darkova, has appeared to have . . . descended into the darkness. She dances with Mazzulah now," the elder said.

A councillor snorted, as another said, "The girl's snapped—she killed her entire guard."

Quinn lifted an eyebrow. "I see," she said. "And what exactly would *I* have to do with this?"

Percinius could only be held silent for so long, it seemed. For he was the next to speak. "Don't act as if you don't know," he hissed, his fingers clenching around the rim of his pedestal as he looked down on her. It was a position he had always possessed—angry, tall, and imposing. Quinn wondered if he had spoken to Risk in that same barely restrained tone as he had raped her half-sister. She wasn't of his blood, but her mere existence was proof of his wife's infidelities. He had no doubt been more violent with Risk than he had ever been with Quinn.

Shards of ice wrapped around her stone heart, every breath she took as she watched him, cutting deeper. She liked the pain. It kept her stable. It made her sane.

"Darkova," Elder Emsworth rose forth, standing from his seat as he never had before, and barked the name at Quinn's father. "You will hold your tongue. This is not a trial."

"If it's not a trial, then what is it?" Quinn asked, curious.

By way of answering, Elder Emsworth raised a palm and curled his long, wrinkled fingers at someone behind her. "Bring forth the girl," he commanded.

The doors at Quinn's back slid open and as she turned, she saw a familiar figure in chains being carted forward. In the light, Loralye looked far worse than she had the night before. Quinn kept her expression blank, her deep-seated satisfaction guarded.

Loralye wasn't a thief, but her actions had stolen time, control, and above all choice, from her and Risk. She had hidden truths—ugly, terrible truths that might not have come to pass if she had been a better sister. A better woman. Risk might not have been imprisoned and raped and starved. Quinn might not have been beaten as often or as harshly. She might not have been sold into slavery had that day at the fountain never happened. But it did.

Loralye now looked as broken and battered as the deeds she'd done as they dragged her through the temple's chancel, coated in dried blood and grime. She reeked of urine. Her once-white shift was torn and one of her breasts on display. Her silver hair was clumped and matted, the color bleeding into a dirty brown where blood had stained its strands.

The guards dropped her before the elder—just a few feet away. When her head jerked up at Quinn, the creature that had once been the proud heir of the Darkova Household let loose a shriek so abominable that it sounded as though it had come from the depths of the Dark Realm.

Quinn didn't even blink as Loralye surged up from her prone position on the stone floors. She tried to scramble back, shaking her head wildly from side to side as if trying to rid herself of the tendrils of fear and anxiety Quinn knew she had left to crawl through the already broken remnants of Loralye's mind.

Councillors cried out, mistaking her movements toward the elders as ones meant to harm, instead of attempts to flee. Soldiers strode forward, intending to snatch her up, but Loralye bolted, evading them all. Quinn pivoted in a circle, staring openly as the woman swayed back and forth.

Soldier's approached from either side, their hands outstretched, speaking in low, gentle tones meant to reassure, but Quinn could see that she didn't hear them. She was already too far gone, just as Quinn had planned for her to be. Lazarus cast a glance between the two sisters before finally letting his attention settle on Loralye and await whatever was about to happen.

Her eldest sister staggered back, mumbling words that were incomprehensible before she began shrieking again. She bumped against a stone pillar and turned toward it abruptly, her hands reaching out and holding fast to its shape.

Loralye's darkness finally rose to the surface and the words Quinn had spoken not a day ago took root. She jerked her head back and slammed it into the pillar, once, twice, three times. The room had gone deathly silent as they watched in collective shock.

Blood dribbled down the stone column and splattered a fresh crimson across the girl's soiled clothes. Brown and red smudged the marbled floors as her dirty feet struggled with balance. The soldiers pulled themselves out of their own dismay and tried to reach for her, to pull her back from what she was doing to herself.

But Loralye wouldn't be stopped.

With a piercing cry that spoke of the pain and torture Quinn had put her through, she flung her head back once more and beat her skull into the pillar so severely that a deafening crack carried through the chamber as she slumped to the ground.

Unmoving at last.

A small spider web fissure marred the surface of the column. The soldiers each looked down at their charge for a moment. Her eyes remained open, staring upward into nothingness as they had while she bashed her own head against the stone. The skin of her forehead was sunken in and split, blood leaked out and down the sides of her face. Red tears streaked against her once pale flesh, already growing ashen in death.

Loralye's mouth hung open beneath her shattered nose, an endless silent scream that echoed into oblivion—never to be heard by another again.

Not a single breath passed through anyone's lips as the room stared down at the bloodied face of what had once been Loralye Darkova, heir to the Darkova House. It was as if sound had simply ceased to exist for a suspended lapse in time. And then, with a rushing explosion, it came back.

"Noooo!" Ethel's scream reverberated up the tall walls of the temple as she crashed to the floor, disappearing from view. Her sobs, however, remained, causing an irritating ache to start pounding in the back of Quinn's skull.

"Take the girl away," Elder Emsworth said, his voice subdued. "Give her body over to the Temple of Telerah. May she have peace." He sounded depleted, as if all of his strength had been sapped from his bones. Quinn turned back as the soldiers bent to their task, lifting Loralye's body and carting it away as if it were nothing more than a heap of garbage meant to be discarded.

Once the husk was gone from the room, Percinius was the first to speak. "Surely, you can see that Quinn is to blame for this, Elder," he said. "Just look at how she reacted."

Elder Emsworth shook his head. "I am truly sorry, Percinius, for both your and Ethel's loss. Your eldest daughter will be missed."

"I do not care about whether or not she shall be missed," Quinn's father raised his voice and slammed a fist down upon his pedestal. "I care about executing the one responsible for her and Edward's death!"

"The person responsible?" Quinn turned her head as a new councillor spoke, recognizing him as Verniez Laltihr. His wife was notably quiet as she stood behind him, staring at the splatter of blood dripping down the column at the front of the room. "The girl was out of her mind," Verniez continued. "No one did anything to her. She was clearly disturbed, likely distraught by her own husband's suicide."

"My daughter would never do what she just did were she not pushed to it," Percinius said over the soft wails of his wife. "I demand you do something,

Elder, as is your duty." He whirled and pointed a finger at Quinn. "Execute her."

Elder Emsworth narrowed his eyes, the low, drooping lids over them hanging lower until his eyes were mere slits in his face. "You wish for me to execute the last remaining heir to the Darkova line? On what grounds?" Percinius opened his mouth, but the elder cut him off before he could say anything more. "We have lost two young souls this very week and I'll not have another destroyed so lightly, not after we have just received her back. She is a blessing of the gods."

Quinn's lips quirked again, but she said nothing, letting her father and the elder work out what would happen. It was already clear to her who held more power, and she knew she would not be held responsible for her sister's death—no matter that it had been at her suggestion, a little whisper in her ear combined with as much fear a body could handle.

"No," Elder Emsworth said again. "I'll not do it."

"Do you not think it curious that these events have taken place upon her return, Elder?" This from Norlinda Sorvent as she and her own husband stared down from their own high place.

Everyone, it seemed, was in attendance this morning.

"What happened was unfortunate, Norlinda," Verniez said. "But you cannot truly believe that the second daughter of the Darkova House would—"

"Believe it?" Amenival squawked. "Why look at her—she looks positively guilty."

Quinn resisted the urge to roll her eyes. Barely.

Verniez sighed and shook his head. "That is ridiculous, Amenival."

"A lot has happened this day. Perhaps we should allow the Darkova House time to grieve before we make any decisions." The suggestion came from the Zandeas woman as she stood watching the others, silent until then.

All heads turned her way, and the elder nodded. "Yes," he agreed. "It has been a trying day, full of sorrow. We shall allow the Darkova House time to grieve. For now, though, the question of the Darkova heir is imperative. It is enough that we have lost an entire house now that both Edward and Loralye Arvis have passed into the beyond without an heir of their own." Elder Emsworth's tired gaze settled on Quinn. "I'll not have another house die out under my guidance. Therefore, it is on this day that I declare Quinn Darkova, second daughter of the Darkova House, as the heir to the Darkova line. What say you, Quinn?"

Percinius straightened as that announcement rang throughout the chancel and Ethel's sobbing took on a high-pitched wail before he reached down and hefted her up. Now, faced with the others in the room instead of hiding away upon the floor beneath her pedestal, the Darkova matriarch cut off her weeping diatribe. Her face was red and swollen, her eyes bloodshot as she blinked about the room. She looked at her husband in confusion as fresh tears descended from her eyes. He bent and hissed something in her ear—Quinn saw the way her eyes widened and snapped to her in horror.

Though Quinn had no notion of staying long enough to remain heir, she stepped forward and bowed her head slightly. In a strong voice that carried her parents' worst nightmare, she responded, "I accept, Elder."

And thus, the next part of her vengeance was struck. Turning to her parents, she leveled both Percinius and Ethel Darkova with a fierce stare. Within it, she promised more than retribution. "I assure you, Mother, Father," she said slowly. "There will be a reckoning for the Darkova House. The gods are indeed just."

Ethel shuddered against Percinius who, for the first time since her return, looked as though he were truly, terribly afraid. As he should be—because despite how the other councillors took her words, as a reassurance and an understanding of their grief, Quinn and her parents knew the truth of it. Vengeance would be had, and their days were not numbered. They were dried up and gone.

Empty

"The world needs darkness, if it stands to see the light."
— *Quinn Darkova, vassal of House Fierté, fear twister,*
white raksasa, heir to the Darkova Household, thoughtful
murderess

Risk clung to her shoulders, her fragile hands still weak, but no longer trembling. While the food and rest she had received since Quinn had rescued her was slowly curing her body, the main source of her strength was her mind. The nightmares that haunted them both. The words said and the deeds done. The horrors that had been dealt to both girls.

They were women now, and for all the things they wished to do, places to go, people they wanted to become . . . there was one final thing to do first.

Quinn pulled her closer as she stepped from the shadows onto the marble porch. The lights inside were dim, almost nonexistent—as if the people inside didn't want to be seen. Didn't want their presence known.

"Are you sure you want this?" Quinn asked her little sister for the first and the last time. "Once we go inside, there's no turning back."

Risk didn't stutter as she answered, firm in her decision. "I'm sure."

"Alright," Quinn said. That was it. The only speaking that would be done between them before it was all over.

Before the ten long, lonely years were finally paid for in reprisal.

She set Risk down and her sister clung to the front wall, leaning into it for support. Her expression was hard—gaze stronger than any man ever could be—as she nodded once for Quinn to start. Dressed in fur-lined pants and a long tunic, she'd been covered from neck to toe and had the thickest cloak Quinn had managed to dig up tied around her. She shivered in the cold. But even that could not dissuade her. Quinn understood. Both of them held an unfathomable, burning fire inside.

Rage kept her warm even when her own body couldn't.

Quinn made quick work of the lock and sheathed the knife. Twisting the handle, it opened easily. The hinges creaked as the wind caught the wood and made it swing open further. Turning, she picked Risk back up before walking inside, shutting the door with a kick of her boot.

The foyer was empty, but a light shined in the living room, casting a light golden glow and shadows in a circle around it.

Quinn walked that distance as silent as the grave she was going to send them to. There was a scraping of chairs and rustle of movements. Her mother appeared in the hallway.

Her pale skin had gone stark white, nearly translucent, but there was no surprise. No, instead there was a different emotion infusing her expression. Terror.

"Get out of my house, you demon!" she snapped, her voice quivering. A second set of footsteps quickly followed behind as her father's face appeared.

"How *dare* you—"

Quinn stopped them both short with a single look. She reached past the distance between them and into their chests, where their hearts of darkness lied. They feared it, that twisted, awful organ that drove them to do terrible things. They lived in the guise of purity, but inside, they were as awful as she. They were every bit as wicked. Their actions just as cruel.

They feared it, though, just as they feared her. Just as they feared Risk.

Her sister trembled slightly, but Quinn knew it had more to do with the dark magic she was using in such close proximity.

Both parents fell to their knees. Her father curled his fingers into claws, trying to fight through the terror and struggle to his feet, trying to move toward her, to stop her. Not that he was able to do much more than flop around on the floor and glare as Quinn's power squeezed inside his chest. Their mother, as weak as she was, succumbed as easily as Loralye, clawing at her eyes and pulling her own hair. Clumps of silver hair slipped from her fingers as she opened her mouth, gasping for air—for relief —for sanity.

Quinn walked past them and neither made a

move to reach for her as she strode by—too absorbed in their own agony. She settled Risk on the lounge. Her sister splayed her fingers across the rough fabric, pulling herself into a sitting position as Quinn retreated back to the foyer. Grabbing her mother by the hair, she dragged her into the living room, binding her wrists behind her back as she did so with a rope she'd brought along for this very purpose. The only fight Ethel Darkova put up was to try to rid herself of the demon in her mind. Not that it would ever happen.

Quinn hadn't simply caused them nightmares. She'd shown them their true, perverted selves. Stripped away was their white robes and pure images. Cast aside were their reputations and name. She showed them the people they were, and they were terrible. Ethel writhed, tears and snot running down her face as she thrashed side to side—too cowardly to attempt killing herself and yet fully consumed in the nightmare. If she were even aware of her daughter's touch, she didn't show it.

Quinn went back for her father, grasping him with both hands by the hem of his robes. She dragged him, flipping him to his back as he contorted inward, curling into a ball—still fighting, and still failing. She bound his wrists as well, and only when they were feet away from the lounge where Risk sat did she pull back from their minds.

Her mother gasped, taking in wild, uncontrolled breaths as she panted hard. Her father looked around. It took mere seconds for the hatred to resettle in his eyes as the fog of pain drifted away, and Quinn took that as a sign that it was time. She slipped the gold-plated brass knuckles over both hands, fitting them just right as she began to speak.

"For years, you've hidden behind your position and your power. You abused your children. You hurt those that didn't deserve your anger. You placed blame where it wasn't due. All because somewhere in your sick, perverted minds, you thought you were right. That you were just." Percinius opened his mouth as Quinn predicted he would.

"What do you think—"

The first hit was like a fissure in the dam that held all the memories behind it. All the reasons for restitution. She slammed the brass knuckles into his jaw, so hard that her father's head whipped back, and he wobbled for a moment, bound as he was on his knees now. Blood splattered the white marble of the Darkova home, and for once, it wasn't hers.

Quinn paused to see if any retaliation came back at her, but all that followed was her father's glare. She felt the power beneath his skin rolling, a beast cracking its eyes open. He held that power at bay, and that just wouldn't do. Quinn sighed, beginning to pace.

"What a pair you both make. The lying, cheating, trust spinner who forced her way into the Council by taking the Darkova name." Her mother lowered her head, tears glistening in her lashes. Quinn didn't care. "And you—*Father*—the tyrant that ruled his family with the strength of a man. You played the part of a perfect councillor, but inside you something was *twisted* and ugly. You beat me for what I am, and after my dear mother had Risk, you took it out on her. Didn't you?"

Something flashed in his eyes as he looked between both girls. Their faces were like stone as they stared back with expressions as damnable as the statues of the gods.

His gaze slowly shifted from Quinn to Risk and she wondered if she saw the way he licked his bottom lip.

"Quinn," Risk said. Her voice remained cold and icy, though she sensed a tremor of fear in her.

She knew what she needed. Him to stop looking at her like that.

Quinn stepped in front of him, blocking his face from view as she looked at her sister.

"He hurt you the most. So, how shall we repay the favor?" Quinn asked her, gentle in her own way.

Risk seemed to consider that as she stared out the back window, her gaze far away. When it cleared, what remained behind was flinty determination. Something merciless settled within her.

"I want him to know how it felt," she whispered. "I want him to hurt as I hurt. To feel pain as I felt pain."

Quinn considered that. "And our mother?" she prompted.

Risk shrugged slightly. "Let her watch, as she watched him with me."

"And then?" Quinn asked.

"Let them die."

Inside her, a sadistic, terrible thrill shot through Quinn's veins as she looked at the man she called her father.

"You know what's going to happen, don't you?" she asked him. He swallowed, and she wondered if he felt true fear. They would know soon enough.

Quinn knelt beside him and leaned in. He eyed her warily as she blew a breath of black magic in his face and let the visions begin.

A darkened cell. Marble floors not so different from those in their living room. Iron bars surrounded him. Chains weighed on his wrists and ankles. She gave him the feeling of starvation but his mind, it created the fear all on its own.

"For ten years you chained her," Quinn said. "I do not have ten years." She lifted a hand and the tendrils drifted into the air before settling on his skin and burrowing deep beneath. Percinius lowered his head, closing his eyes tightly. He didn't realize that closing his eyes or opening them: it wouldn't matter in the end. He'd see and feel and live exactly as Risk had. "The mind is an interesting thing. It can play tricks on you. A minute can turn into an eternity with the right push. That's what I'm going to do to you. I'll push and push, until you shatter." Percinius quivered. "Let's begin."

In his mind, she led him through the motions of being taken from his cell and placed upon an altar. They strapped him down with his front against the stone. His body bare. Two hands parted his cheeks and something blunt entered him from behind.

She wanted to draw out that first initial invasion. Quinn reveled in his pain, knowing that he finally understood what his repayment for abuse would be.

Percinius jerked.

"No," he moaned, as the feeling of being assaulted overcame him. The line between real and imagined had become blurry. He wouldn't tell the difference.

"Just remember, Father, you brought this on yourself," she mocked, reminding him of his own words.

"No, no," he started to thrash but his wrists were bound. The imaginary man sped up and finished inside him. Percinius stilled for a moment.

She called forth another invisible man he'd never seen. And when this one began to rape him anew, Percinius screamed.

"Please stop," he sobbed. "Please . . ."

"You're evil," Quinn said. "Wicked." He shuddered as the second man finished and a third came. His mind slowly beginning to unravel. "This is not even close to understanding what it's like to be powerless. Used. Abused. But you're beginning to understand." Blood vessels burst in his face. His eyes turning red where they were white. He screamed so loud, but the neighbors would not hear it. No one would. Except her, and Risk, and their mother.

She did this again and again, till his screams echoed in the cold, empty house and his voice cracked and then grew hoarse, becoming barely more than a whisper as he pleaded for it to stop. Their mother begged as well, but neither daughter answered.

Quinn drew it out, making each individual minute span out and last.

She walked him through the initial night and then captivity after. She let shadow men visit him in his cell and rape him there, on the floor, bound like an animal. Physically she never touched him, but mentally—he was broken.

Risk observed every second of it, enraptured by the brutality, captivated by the reparations paid. Ramiel, the God of Justice, reveled in the age-old belief in taking an eye for an eye, and so, now did she.

Quinn paid her father back for every transgression and then some, all the while reaping his memories and stealing his fears. She garnered faces and names, but they were for later, for what came last.

Only when the fight had completely left him,

and he'd stopped screaming, stopped crying, stopped trying to get away, did Quinn actually stop.

Percinius didn't move.

"Has he paid for his crimes?" Quinn asked her sister.

"No," Risk answered, staring at him. The light coming from the fireplace made her blue eyes seem brighter. Her skin look warmer. "But he will. The dark realm awaits him."

Quinn looked at Risk and felt something in her chest tighten. It was only when she pulled the knife from its sheath that she felt it then.

Dark magic, stretching its clawed hands out.

Whispers of fear—the power of it—that were not her own.

Quinn smiled and reached around behind him and cut the bindings on his wrists. The hatred he had for her was greater than any she'd ever known, but that hatred wasn't there anymore. Replaced with fury was a fear so great that while he lashed out to protect himself, he wouldn't even lift a hand when given the chance. Quinn still crouched in front of him, she gave her father a wide, unbelieving grin.

"There it is," she whispered. "For so many years you told me that *I* was the reason mother was disturbed. That *I* was the cause for her turning to a raksasa. You told me *I* was evil, and *I* was corrupt. You told me you wished you'd killed me when I still rested within her womb." Percinius said nothing, though Ethel wailed so loud the dark realm might have heard it. "You and I are alike, though, aren't we, Father? I think you knew that even all those years ago. You hated me because your magic is the same that runs in my veins. You hid your darkness, pretending to play in the light. You made it twisted. Perverted. Evil." Quinn lifted the dagger to his throat, lightly skimming it. A trail of scarlet slid down the blade. "I was only a child then, but your actions led me here—and when the darkness claims you, I pray that you find no peace in it. You don't deserve death, but I am tired. I've held onto this for ten years, and now it's time to let go—or I would become what I hate more than all else. You."

Then, she did the unexpected. Quinn lowered the knife and offered him the hilt. His eyes, blown wide, looked from it to her. "Go ahead," she whispered. "Take it."

Sweat-slicked fingers reached out tentatively. He grasped the knife in a shaking grip. "That's it," she encouraged. "Now lift your robe."

Percinius frowned, the panic beginning to stir once more.

Still, he lifted his robe.

"Higher," she commanded.

He did so.

"Very good. Now grab it—and cut it off."

Percinius paused and looked at her. His lips parted. Quinn leaned forward and whispered again, "Cut it off. Now."

Percinius began to rock himself. His fisted hand moving to the end of his length, holding it as he lowered the knife. Its edge pressed down and a thin line of crimson welled against the blade and trickled over. Percinius grit his teeth in agony as Ethel screamed for him to stop. To not do it. She told him that he didn't want this. That he didn't wish to die.

But Ethel couldn't have been more wrong.

After experiencing the torture in his mind, those few hours felt like months—years—and he was ready. Unlike Risk—who was so strong she persevered over a decade, fought to live, and sat here now, watching the monster castrate himself—Percinius was not strong. He was weak of mind and body. He was nothing.

Percinius pushed harder with the knife, its edge

sliding cleanly through. Tears ran down his face as he screamed and sobbed, gripping the bloody dagger with one hand and his dismembered organ with the other.

Blood spurted, running in rivulets down his legs. Red blossomed in his robes, the cotton fabric soaking in his life's blood as the blade slipped from his fingers. He opened his mouth to scream again, but his voice was already gone. Only a silent, choking rasp emitted from him as he fell back.

"Now lie there and die," Quinn said icily. His body had barely touched the cold ground when she turned to their mother.

"Your turn."

She picked the dagger up off the floor and clenched the bloodied handle in her grip. Quinn stepped around her father, whose wide, glassy eyes stared up at the ceiling without seeing. Ethel sobbed into her robes, tears and snot running down her face.

"Please," she said. "I didn't do anything—I didn't rape—"

"You also didn't stop them," Quinn said harshly. "For that, we won't stop him."

Ethel's face blanched. Her lips turned colorless. "No," she whispered as the vision started to take her. "Please, anything but that—" She didn't get to finish the sentence as Quinn gave her a reality too close to their own. She could still see both her daughters. She knew she was in her living room. She saw Percinius' body, bleeding out on the pristine floor.

But in her mind she saw his corpse lift the dead organ in his hand and settle it upon its stump. The body of the man sat up and turned his once again hateful eyes on his wife. Ethel's jaw slipped ajar. If she'd been paying attention, she might have noted the scent of damp petals and midnight weeds. As it was, her dead husband stood and grabbed her by the hair. She didn't react. She didn't have time to before he pushed that organ between her lips.

Her face turned red and her eyes puffy as she snapped out of it and tried to push him away. He pried her jaw open with his large hand and wrapped the other in her hair, taking his pleasure without a care for his wife. When he was done, he cast her away. And though she remained in the same place, her mind thought her body was sprawled on the floors as her husband then held her down, his shaft growing thick again as he raped her.

Quinn thought she would scream. That she would cry. Instead she shut down. Her expression shuddered closed as she took it. Her arms shook but she did not fight as deep in her thoughts as he did what he desired. Her head did not thrash. Her legs did not kick. She might as well have been as dead as the corpse fucking her.

When it was over, several times later, Quinn vanished the illusion from her mother's mind.

Ethel's eyes didn't clear. Unseeing as Loralye had been, she sat there on her knees and stared at the fissures in the marble floor. Quinn approached again, crouching in front of her. She leaned in and put her lips to her mother's ear, her other hand going around to cut the ties that still bound her wrists.

"You are a horrid person, and an even more wretched mother. Your husband is dead. Your children are either dead or hate you. There is nothing left for you in this world," Quinn whispered.

"There's nothing left for me . . . of me . . ." her mother murmured back.

"When the sun rises, you will take this knife and slit your own throat, won't you?" She lifted the metal piece and Ethel focused on it and began trembling again. "If you don't, I'll bring him back. I'll let him do this to you for the rest of your life. You understand, don't you?"

Whatever fear in her eyes that remained died out instantly. She was resigned, and Quinn knew the job would be done.

She stood and turned, leaving the knife on the end table. Ethel watched it and only it. Her pale fingers clenching and unclenching.

"I understand," she said.

"Good."

It would be done. With Percinius already dead and her mind as gone as Loralye's had been, Ethel Darkova would do anything to be rid of her fear, her husband, herself.

Quinn looked down at the last of her vengeance before it slipped from this world and all she felt was . . . emptiness. The feeling didn't sit well, that after so long of holding onto the hate—there was nothing left when her revenge had been seen through and she no longer had it.

Smooth, bony fingers grasped hers.

She looked down at her sister. They were both dry-eyed but there was something in the air that she couldn't put a name to.

"Let's go," Risk told her.

Quinn picked up Risk, this time carrying her against her front. Her sister embraced her with open arms, clinging to her tight as they braved the cold of night once again.

Tonight, there was no howl of the wind. No shriek of frigid air. The sky had all but cleared, and the stars looked down on them.

"It's over," Risk said as the house they were staying in came into view. Quinn hiked down the sloping hill and up the steps.

"No," she said as they went inside and headed straight up to her room. "They're over. Our time here is over—but we're not."

She laid Risk on the bed and crawled in beside her. They didn't hug, but they held hands as they laid on their sides, facing each other. "Do you feel it?" Risk asked.

Quinn frowned. "Feel what?"

It hadn't been long, but Risk was already slipping into sleep as she whispered, "Peace."

Her lips parted as she realized that was what was missing.

That feeling that still eluded her after all these years.

Peace.

Why was it that she carried out her plans, yet it was emptiness that claimed her and not peace? Why was it that even here, in her darkest moments, she didn't feel whole? Quinn assumed after so long of not belonging, that it was vengeance that would fix her—that she would feel something—anything —other than the emptiness in her heart.

A quiet knock came at the door. She knew who it was.

Him.

Quinn slipped from the bed and into the hallway. Shutting the door softly behind her.

"I trust it's done?" Lazarus asked her.

"It's done." She nodded, silently extending her hand. Neiss slipped from her skin and settled in the hall at her side, growing in size. "I got the names. I know the faces. He will lead you to them."

She turned to retreat back inside, but a light touch ghosted her back—rough fingers along her spine giving her pause. The scent of wildfires and smoke washed over her as Lazarus whispered, "You will never be like them—because inside you are so much more. Your darkness shines brighter than any light."

She turned, but he was already striding away, Neiss slithering after him.

She'd promised herself that the streets of N'skara would run red upon her return, and tonight, she kept that promise. But it was that ghost of a touch that lured her to a final, dreamless sleep, like the shadow of an emotion she'd sought for so long.

A shadow that would forever plague her, as nameless as it was impossible to refuse.

Violent Justice

"Ramiel judges all in his own time."
— *Draeven Adelmar, vassal of House Fierté, rage thief*

I ce crunched under Draeven's boots as he
pivoted and scanned the street. His breath
puffed in front of his face, a white cloud hanging
over his vision for a moment before clearing. The
night was a bitter cold and Draeven tilted his head
toward Leviathan's eye, sucking the chill into his
lungs. It didn't take a seer Maji to determine that
the night would soon be filled with the scent of
blood. It had only just begun.

The screams that had come from within the

Darkova house made him shudder, and though he prided himself on being a man of transparency, he had no desire to know what had transpired behind that door. He would rather remain in blissful ignorance if only for a little longer. For several hours he and Dominicus had stood guard while Quinn meted out her revenge. When the front door opened again, Quinn walked away and didn't look back.

While evil people they were, Quinn was a different kind of woman unto herself. It took a hard person, a strong person, to kill two people—let alone her parents—and never look back. He and Dominicus followed her as she carried her sister through the streets of Liph at a remarkably swift pace. They stayed close enough to watch, but not be seen by the other girl. The one he'd yet to get a real look at because she huddled so close to Quinn that with the cloak, she was unidentifiable if not for the lavender-haired woman.

Quinn went inside. They remained in the cold while they waited for their lord. After a few moments, the front door opened, and Lazarus appeared. He made his way over to them.

"What are your orders?" Draeven inquired.

Lazarus met his left-hand's calm stare. "Three

more men will die tonight," he said. "They have participated in the worst of crimes—torture, unlawful imprisonment, and rape." Draeven's back stiffened for a moment at the mention of the latter. Anger ripped through him, destroying every singular thought in his mind except that of violence. *Rape*.

Draeven had committed many sins in his life, but none so great as that. To rape a woman was to defile someone in an irreparable way. He'd seen the damage firsthand. When his own sister had been raped and then slaughtered. Pulling himself back from the brink took a moment and he almost missed his lord's next words. "N'skara still has much to offer me," Lazarus continued. "But these men do not. They will die tonight. No trial."

"It shall be done," Draeven swore, bowing his head. His fingers portrayed a fine tremble with his barely contained rage as he folded his hand into a fist and pressed it over his chest.

"Whatever is required of me will be done." Dominicus did the same.

"Good." Lazarus turned and gestured down an alleyway to where a mauve-colored basilisk awaited. "Follow the snake and we will mete out the justice that is deserved."

The three of them moved, one after the other, following after the scaled animal as it slithered through the snow. Fury still pulsed beneath Draeven's flesh as he stared ahead, fixing his gaze on the back of Lazarus' head. Draeven wondered, idly, if Lazarus had told them the crimes of these men specifically for this reason. He was not one to say something without meaning, without reason. Surely, Lazarus had known that this would be Draeven's reaction. Now, even if his master commanded him to stand back, it would be near impossible for Draeven to resist the urge to find and kill these men.

They passed through the ghostly city, striding through the shadows. Even with the light of the moon to illuminate their path, the city, it seemed, was cloaked in a heavy layer of mist and gloom, aiding them in their movements. Finally, Lazarus stopped at a three-way fork in the road.

Twisting, Lazarus glanced over his shoulder and met Draeven's gaze once more. "The creature claims that one of the men lives at the end of this path. He is from the Council. Look for an opulent house with a crest on it. I trust you to know how to find your target?"

Draeven merely nodded and broke off from the

group just as Lazarus addressed Dominicus next. Draven did not stick around to hear what else was said. He'd been given his instructions. And even with the lack of a map or knowledge of what the rapist looked like, it was not a difficult task for Draeven.

He stopped before a wide house with columns of white. A crest of pure gold was mounted above the door, though it was too dark to clearly make out. All around it, the buildings seemed to lead to this one, as if whoever lived in this mansion was far more important. Draeven felt a deceptive stillness fall over him as he reached for the hilt of his sword and unsheathed the weapon. Draeven found an opening in the back—a weak door with an anti-quated locking mechanism that was easily picked. The door clicked and swung open silently.

It was the same everywhere he went. Those who often had held power for too long soon thought of themselves as invincible.

This man was the same, and he would die for it.

The house was quiet. Silent as the grave as he ascended a staircase and found his way to the sleeping chambers. Expensive portraits hung from the walls and Draeven paused by them as he passed. A man with sagging jowls and drooping lids was depicted on each one. Often dressed in a robe of white that mimicked those he had seen people wear in the streets of Liph since his arrival, the man in the images was always alone. Draeven could only pray that meant he had no wife and no children. Not that it would have swayed him from his purpose after what Lazarus had told him, but if he could be spared the grief of family members, that would be a true blessing from the gods.

Continuing forward, Draeven listened quietly. His footsteps were muted against luxurious rugs meant to keep the floor from retaining the same chill that seeped in through the windows and doors. Soft snores reached his ears and Draeven followed them until he reached the bedroom from which the sounds emitted. Cracking the door, Draeven slipped inside on hushed feet and stopped once more.

In a four-poster bed, lay a giant of a man— thick in the middle and rumbling with his snores. This was the man from the portraits. His target. Draeven was not the type to kill a defenseless man, much less a man unaware of his very presence. Turning his blade, Draeven tapped the flat end against one of the end posts of the bed roughly. The dull thuds echoed up, startling the man from his dreams.

The man woke with a start, spluttering. He sat up in his bed. Draeven waited as the man's vision cleared, and he fixed the stranger standing in his room with a mixture of shock and irritation, until he saw the sword in Draeven's hand. He began to speak, then yell.

Though Draeven couldn't understand the N'skari language, it did not take a translator for Draeven to understand. Scanning the room, he spotted a rack aligned next to a stone hearth across from the bed. Striding over, Draeven withdrew one of the fire pokers and swung back to the vile man, who had half-crawled from his bed.

Draeven tossed the poker at the man's feet. It was a crude weapon, but Draeven had been kind enough to give him at least the opportunity to defend himself, though he knew it was futile. *Maybe I should have killed the man in his sleep*, Draeven thought. *It would have been over and done and he wouldn't have had to suffer.* But then again . . . this creature, this rapist hadn't cared for the harm he'd caused to someone else.

"Pick up your weapon," Draeven ordered, pointing the end of his sword to the poker at the fat man's feet.

With brows drawn down in bewilderment, the

man merely followed the path of Draeven's gesture. Slowly he reached down, keeping an eye on the blade before him, the man grasped for the poker. As soon as his fingers closed over the iron metal, Draeven struck. It was a moment of pure instinct that kept the man's head from rolling as his weighty body swayed, but his arm lifted just enough to block Draeven's sword from its aim—the man's throat.

Crying out in agony, the man's arm fell away from his body. Blood gushed forth, splattering across the tops of Draeven's boots. The man howled in pain, his free hand dropping the iron poker and grasping at the stump of his arm. Draeven's gaze landed on the severed limb as it dropped onto the plush rug beneath his feet.

The man scrambled back. It was obvious he was no fighter. He didn't even spare the forgotten iron poker a glance as he cried and sobbed. Words fell from his lips.

They were pleas for mercy, and Draeven knew that because they were always pleas no matter the language they spoke. Draeven was sure that the woman that this man had violated had likely also begged in the same fashion and he doubted any sort of sympathy had even crossed his mind. There would be no benevolence from him. No forgiveness. No leniency.

In that dark room in the coldest country on the Sirian Continent, Draeven exacted vengeance. It took one swipe for the man's jugular to be severed. The creature coughed and sputtered. A few droplets landed on Draeven's cheek, one sliding down toward his chin as he yanked his sword back and prepared for his final swing. The second and last blow ended the man's life. As his sobs cut off, the night grew silent once more.

In the End

"There is no changing what has been, but what will be is still within your grasp."
— *Quinn Darkova, vassal of House Fierté, fear twister, white raksasa, heir to the Darkova Household, content murderess*

A *nd so it ends.*

It was the singular thought that circled Quinn's mind the following day as she and Lazarus climbed the steps of the Council's temple. The white morning sun left a blanket of duskiness over the rest of the eerie city. It was well past time for the early risers to be up and about, but unsurprisingly, the streets were a veritable ghost town.

There was a cast of fear stretching from inside the temple archway and Quinn followed the strands as they called to her, stepping into the chancel with cries of outrage and panic lifting with every voice that entered the conversation. Lazarus stood at Quinn's back, a tall behemoth of grim stillness as they watched the councillors argue amidst each other, their faces tight with worry and anxiety.

One by one, as the remaining councillors realized their presence. Heads turned toward them, and voices fell quiet. "Good morning," Quinn said once she held all of their attentions. More silence greeted her in turn and Quinn took a short walk forward, striding until she found the stairway to the side that led up to the podiums from which they sat.

She ascended those steps and found the Darkova seat, settling herself comfortably in the front most position as Lazarus trailed her and took up residence at the smaller seat just behind her. It was dwarfed by his massive frame, but after shifting for a moment, he merely leaned into it and crossed his arms, surveying the rest of the room.

Quinn took a breath. "As you are all now aware,"

she began, "last night, three highborn Houses, all from the Council, suffered some rather unfortunate circumstances." Quinn's gaze spanned the room, landing on a white-faced Norlinda Sorvent. She stared at both Quinn and Lazarus in utter horror and her husband, who had usually sat just behind her, was notably absent. *As he should be*, Quinn thought. "You are all that's left. I would count yourselves lucky."

"Quinn Darkova." Elder Emsworth's voice was the first to reply and as Quinn turned her face his way, waiting expectantly, he opened his mouth to continue. However, even as his lips parted, questions and confusion whirled in the depths of his glazed sea blue eyes. He didn't know where to begin. What questions to ask. Why she was sitting before them now.

"I'm sure you're wondering why," Quinn said, answering the unspoken queries. She glanced over them all and several nodded their heads submissively, most avoiding her gaze directly. She nodded, satisfied. "The answer is simple." Quinn placed her hands on the edge of the pedestal, standing as her nails scored the undersides with her grip. "This Council has taken something from me and my family that can never be given back. There is no amount of compensation that can pay for what has been so brutally stolen."

Every single face in the chamber was confused, apart from Lazarus and her own. That was good because their confusion was the very reason they were alive. The remaining members—the Elder, Norlinda Sorvent, Verniez Laltihr and his wife, and the Zandeas House had been blind to the ways of the others. The missing members were dead. Each remaining name had been a thought in her father's head the night before as she'd let the fear she held power over infiltrate him. All of his memories had been spread out for her perusal. Even though Risk hadn't been able to name all of her abusers, Percinius had. After the exhaustion of ending him, she'd simply left the rest of them to Lazarus.

What he and Draeven and Dom did thereafter, she'd never know.

They were dead and that was all that mattered.

"I-If there's no manner of compensation that can pay for . . . whatever it is that we've done, how is it that half of our Council is dead?"

Quinn flipped her attention to the speaker, Verniez's wife, as she half-cowered behind her husband. Quinn didn't mind the question. She intended to answer it, in fact, but not before she made it quite clear what it was that they had done.

"Ten years ago, I was not snatched away by slave traders from the south," she said, her voice rising in volume so that all could hear the tale. "I was sold." She paused at the audible gasp that ran through the Council. Satisfied that they realized the weight of her claim, she continued. "I was sold into slavery by your very own Percinius and Ethel Dark-ova. Over ten years I had seventeen masters, each who burned their own brand into my skin." She reached for the ties on her cloak and the thick fur piece fell, pooling at her feet. Quinn turned and raised her hair, showing them the Xs that marked her back from the most brutal whipping she'd ever received. "For ten years I was a slave to be bought and beaten and used for men beyond these borders because my parents deemed me evil for something I could not control." She lowered her hair and turned back to them. "You hold Maji in high regard, but only those chosen by the light. The gray are still to be respected, but the black? We do not choose our magic; our magic chooses us. I was chosen by the dark and I paid for that. I paid a price that was not owed," her voice rose, letting that proclamation hang there for a moment. "But I am not the only one. My younger half-sister by Ethel Darkova was secreted away as well shortly after they sold me. Until then, she had lived her life as a servant in the Darkova House. But for the next ten years as I fought my way back here, she was chained and caged in a temple outside of Liph for the sole manner of being tortured and raped by members of the Council every single day."

A gasp of horror rose up and Norlinda Sorvent wavered on her feet, her hands going out to clutch her pedestal. She and several other members looked ready to either vomit or faint. Elder Emsworth was the only one whose expression remained closed off. Quinn eyed him as she continued.

"I set out to rescue my sister from prison and kill those responsible. Last night, my objective reached its end." Quinn looked down at the pin she had worn for just this purpose. The Council's pin for the Darkova House, marking her as an heir to a seat among them. She ripped the offending piece of metal from the furred wrap and tossed it into the empty section of the chancel. The pin fell, all eyes following it briefly, before they returned to Quinn. The metal pin clanged loudly against the stone, and she spoke again. "The N'skari Council as you've known it is no more."

"What now, then?" Elder Emsworth finally asked, rasping across the muted room. "What happens next?" She looked at him and he shook his head, standing from his seat, his limbs shaking with the effort. A lower born servant with wide, terrified eyes looked to him and then to Quinn. The boy wanted to help, but was too afraid to move. She nodded his way and with a quick dart, the boy was at the elder's side, taking one arm gently as he helped the old man stand and move forward. "You've killed half of the ruling Houses in the span of a few short days, but without a ruling body, there is nothing left," the old man said. "Chaos will reign —unless you expect to stay here and rule in our stead?"

Quinn shook her head. "Of course not. I never intended to stay. I agreed to think about it and think about it, I have. The solution is simple. You will remain behind and rule as you always have. A smaller Council will still be effective, perhaps more so now that the corruption you've suffered from within has been permanently removed."

"You expect that we'll simply continue on as we always have?" he asked, shocked, leaning heavily on the boy. "And once you're gone, we'll . . . what? Simply forgive and forget?"

A smile overtook her face. "I do not care if you find forgiveness for me, Elder," she said slowly so that the meaning of her words sank in. "I look for no forgiveness. You'll rule as you have, but you will also accept an alliance with Lazarus Fierté of Norcasta."

"And what's to keep us from reneging on that if you'll not stay?" he shot back. *Cantankerous old man,* Quinn thought with weary amusement.

"You'll accept his authority and sign a blood contract with him." She paused and looked to the rest of the Council. "Each of you will swear a blood contract with him that, if broken, will result in your deaths."

"A-and if we refuse?" This from Councillor Laltihr.

His question was met with a calculated glare. "Then you forfeit your life," Quinn said. "But the time to make your decision is now."

"There is no decision to be made," Verniez said quietly as he raised a hand to his wife, easing the woman back as he descended from his pedestal and strode to the center of the chancel, facing up to Quinn as Lazarus stood and joined her at the edge. "You've ensured that."

Lifting a brow, she shook her head in disagreement. "I've given you all far more choice than my sister or I ever received."

He watched her carefully before nodding. "Yes, you're right. I suppose you have. I'm sorry for what happened to your sister, and to you. Just as you don't seek forgiveness, I do not expect you to give it. It is our responsibility to keep our people safe, even children from their own parents. We failed you both and I understand that. I won't fail another as grievously as we have you. I'll sign with Lord Fierté and vow to uphold it."

"Verniez!" Norlinda hissed. "You're not serious."

"Oh, but I am," he said. "Unlike you, I have a family left to protect and if I must do this to keep them safe, then I will. Even if the flames of the dark realm consume my eternal soul, I will have kept them protected—and serve our people still."

A sharp spike of something Quinn couldn't name shot through her and she felt a tightness behind her eyes. She felt anger for some reason, that he wanted to protect his family. That they came first. She couldn't understand why, so she pushed it aside. Pivoting, Quinn, too, descended into the chancel, moving until she stood face-to-face with Councillor Verniez Laltihr. Reaching out, she let a tendril of darkness slip from her grasp and encircle him. Several others gasped as he stiffened—the realization of what she was revealed to them. But Quinn didn't seek to harm, merely to judge, and what she found in the councillor was honesty and truth. She withdrew from him nearly as quickly as she had entered before she looked up to Lazarus and nodded.

"It's time," she said so that he could understand her. "They've agreed to the blood contract. Call forth the firedrake."

Lazarus nodded and within moments, a bird of great beauty—its feathers red and burning—descended as he pulled on the power that he held within. Quinn took a step back and even though she felt the stares of the councillors, she let her stare focus mainly on Verniez Laltihr as he was the first to swear loyalty to Lazarus. The others soon followed, even the Elder as the servant at his side helped him down into the main chancel to receive his brand.

She watched it all with a feeling of detachment, following Verniez with a curiosity as he turned and went to his wife, holding her when she, too, received her brand of loyalty and spoke her own oath. There was a feeling of strange envy she felt at watching him. She had a feeling that had he been her father, and Risk's, the events of the world that had unfolded would have been much different. There were so few people with souls such as his—he reminded her of Draeven in a way, as annoying as Lord Sunshine could be.

"Quinn?" She startled at the sound of her own name. Lazarus appeared at her side as the others quietly rubbed their places of branding as the black mark of their new master's name disappeared beneath their skin. "Are you ready?"

She nodded. "Yes."

With that, she and Lazarus exited the Council's temple for the last time. As they slipped down the front steps, her head tilted back toward the sky as it brightened, and a lone bird cried out—shooting from the tip of the temple roof to span its great black wings and take flight—heading south.

A single drop of blood fell from the bird's feathers, crushed into the snow from the sole of Quinn's boots as she and Lazarus headed back the way they had come.

And so it ends, she thought once more.

Nostalgia's Price

*"Even those who live in the dark desire to be longed for and
understood, foolhardy as those feelings are."*
— Quinn Darkova, vassal of House Fierté, fear twister,
white raksasa, heir to the Darkova Household, pensive
murderess

The scent of alcohol tinged the air, along with
a certain infectious joy that Lazarus' party
was partaking in. Axe was on her fourth or fifth pint
of orange liquor. Where she got it, no one knew, but
neither were they asking questions. Lorraine and
Dominicus sat in the corner, looking deep in
conversation while they sipped their tea. Vaughn

and Draeven were playing a hand of cards, some game from the far lands of Bangratas. Draeven was conveniently winning, but then, he was also teaching the mountain man as he went.

The atmosphere would feel almost normal were it not for the heavy thoughts that weighed on Quinn this night. It was their last day in N'skara and tomorrow they'd all be on their way—to better lands, brighter futures. But on this night there was something in the air that only Quinn could feel. That nameless emotion that evaded her in the late hours, whereas it seemed that everyone had it in abundance. She couldn't name what it was. She didn't truly understand.

It was that lack of being able to empathize with their merriment that had her striding away. Upstairs, Risk was fast asleep, Neiss curled around her. They had a big day tomorrow and she had no desire to wake her sister when she needed all the rest in a warm bed that she could get. The journey would be long and hard for one of her frailty. But she knew deep down, that even if that were not the case, she still wouldn't go to Risk.

Whatever it was that sat on her shoulders tonight was something that they couldn't understand, not any of them, for while they dabbled in the darkness for one reason or another—Quinn lived in it.

She slipped out the front door, forgoing a cloak. The skies had settled, and the winds had calmed. It seemed that truly everyone and everything was at peace tonight—but her.

That thought soured in her stomach as she pushed her lips together and began walking. Aimlessly she allowed her feet to carry her without thought of where or why. She trailed along the silent streets paying no mind to much of anything at all as she came to stop before a house.

The wrought iron gate looked particularly menacing that night, not that it bothered her. She stared at the front door of her childhood home and hesitated. Her fingers were only inches from the metal handle, but something made her pause.

Last night she'd murdered her parents here and told herself she wouldn't be back. She never thought she'd see these doors again, but for some reason her subconscious led her here of all the places. She didn't think too hard on it because she didn't want to.

Quinn grasped the handle and turned. It swung open without effort. The creak of its hinges cast an eerie feeling over her as she strolled into the foyer—

her steps slowing as she came to a halt in the living room.

She had to give it to them. The N'skari cleaned meticulously. Her parents' corpses were gone, and the crimson stain wiped clean. Not a speck of blood was in sight despite the way she'd made it run. *Rivers*, she told herself. *I dreamed of rivers*.

But even rivers could run dry in a drought.

The spotless marble flooring only served to darken her mood.

She wanted to paint them red again and again and again. With a start, Quinn realized that emptiness had evaded her if only for that brief moment where the dark creeped in.

Rage. Pain. Anger. Those things made her heart beat and her blood thrum with life. She never felt more herself as she did when she was enacting her revenge. But when it was all over, all she'd felt was empty. She hated that. The vast chasm that opened in her chest making it difficult to pretend—to act like she were normal. But in that short lapse of time, she felt something stir again. As soon as she looked upon the cleansed floors, it was gone.

She cursed under her breath, turning for the stairs. She took them one at a time, stopping at the third one from the top as it dipped and the whole thing let out a groan. She'd played on these stairs as a child and when her parents argued, her and Risk sat on the top two, so they could eavesdrop without anyone knowing.

Those memories still filled her with a strange sort of comfort as she reached the upper platform and looked at the closed door directly in front of her. She reached for this handle. Her fingers trembled. She wouldn't let that stop her as something greater than curiosity drove her. She opened the door and if the memories were bad before—they swarmed her now.

Ghosts of a child's laugh filled her ears as she saw little silver-haired girls running from the bed to the window. A child form of herself unlatched the silver lock and swung the pane open, fearlessly climbing out onto the roof. Risk followed her and they stayed out half the night before the cold became too bitter to withstand. Pink-cheeked and windblown, they crawled into bed. Risk wasn't supposed to sleep with her. Her parents wanted her to sleep with the other servants in the basement, but they rarely checked and neither girl wanted to be alone.

The memory was so vivid in her mind that Quinn stumbled for a moment, her fingers latching onto a child's dresser to maintain her balance. She'd hated so much about this house, but this room—her room—was not one of those things. The best parts of her childhood took place in here, building forts and enacting pirate battles using one of Percinius' canes she stole and her mother's wooden spoons.

The staircase let out a groan, but Quinn didn't turn.

Only one man would be able to make it that far in her parents' home without her notice. The scent of smoke and wildfire suffused her, laced with traces of bourbon and something else. Something she couldn't so much as name or smell, but it was there in the air, drawing him closer. She shivered, but it was not cold.

"You followed me," Quinn stated, looking out her window to the moon high over dark waters.

"Are you surprised?" he asked.

"No," she answered as he stepped around her, coming into view.

He nodded, taking in the room. She wasn't sure how she felt about him being in the only space she ever claimed as hers, despite the house now being her inheritance as well. Quinn was a wealthy woman, not that she planned to do anything but leave it to rot.

"The others are celebrating," Lazarus said after a long moment.

"I know."

He looked back to her, that heavy gaze all fire and ash. Lazarus was a savage creature forced to live in a human skin, but it was his eyes that showed her what he really was.

Something like her.

"Yet you're here?" he asked softly, but not gently. Not warm. "Why?"

Quinn swallowed but her mouth felt dry. She looked past him to the room around her, the answer coming unbidden to her lips. "Because I don't understand it. I can't relate. I understand logically why they're celebrating, but whatever it is that lets them feel so . . . relieved. I don't understand that."

"So you left?" Lazarus asked, a darker note entering his voice.

"Why are you prying?" Quinn shot back, narrowing her gaze.

"Because I want to know. I want to understand."

Quinn sighed and looked away. "Usually it doesn't bother me, but for some reason I find myself frustrated that I can't be at peace like them. That no matter where I am or who I kill—whatever it is that lets them enjoy their lives so easily—I don't feel that."

Lazarus took a step toward her, and it was the difference between being a chasm apart and mere inches. "What do you feel?" he asked her.

"I . . ." She paused, her eyes slowly rising to meet his. "I thought that killing them would cool this rage, but I'm beginning to think that nothing will. Nothing but more killing, more violence, more . . . games." She wanted to look away, because the truth was an ugly thing. His gaze held her captive though, so she continued. "I told myself for so long that the ends will justify any means, and yet . . ."

"Yet?" he prompted.

"Nothing has changed. If anything—I crave it now that I know how it feels. The feel of blood between my fingers and the look in a man's eyes as death is upon him—" she stopped herself short. There were some things that were better left unsaid and the feelings gnawing at what little remained of her heart were exactly that—but Lazarus wanted them. He wanted it all.

"Keep going," he told her.

"I don't want to become some diplomat or be confined by the courts of Norcasta upon return. I don't think I can. Not . . . after everything that's happened." She took a steady breath and said, "You awakened a monster when you took me, and it has no intentions of going back to the bars that society wants to cage it in."

Lazarus lifted a hand to her face, his palm calloused but warm as it slid down her cheek, his fingers locking around her chin. Their breath mingled and he said, "I have no intentions of caging you, Quinn. You're beautiful and glorious as you are." Her eyebrows started to draw together. "Draeven is my left-hand. He'll be the diplomat, and I the king. But you—you'll be my right-hand. The hand that strikes. You already are."

"And if I do something that you deem going too far?" she asked. "What then?"

A heavy pause passed before Lazarus spoke.

"Then I'll punish you." She lifted an eyebrow and his hand dropped away.

"Punish me?" she asked, tearing herself away finally. She looked to the ceiling and laughed once. "Do you realize how laughable I find that?" Quinn asked caustically. Her voice taunting. Mocking him.

"I'm going to be king," came his reply. "What do you expect? If you go too far, I'll find a way to guide you back—but I won't cage you. I won't—"

He stopped short, cursing under his breath. Quinn stepped away, her expression going cold.

"A cage of your making is still a cage," Quinn replied icily.

"And what would you have me do?" Lazarus asked her. He motioned around them. "All of this was for my crown. We came here for my crown. I let you play your games, Quinn, but I won't have you jeopardizing—"

"Your beloved crown," she said scathingly. "Yes, I know. You care more about a hunk of metal than anyone or anything in your life. I might be empty, Lazarus, only able to come alive when I play my games—but what about you? When you have the crown and it's all over and you've reached your goals—what will you have?"

He didn't answer, and Quinn smiled.

"Mark my words, it won't be enough for you." She threw her arms wide. "You can have as many alliances as you want, but just like me—you'll get your crown—and you'll feel empty inside. You're just too much of a fool to see it—"

He came at her so fast she didn't have time to react as a hand so hot it nearly burned her skin wrapped around her throat. He squeezed, but only in warning as he pushed her back against the wall.

"What did I tell you about calling me a fool?" His voice was deadly, and her pulse raced at the violence in it.

"What are you going to do about it, Lazarus?" she asked hoarsely. "Punish me?"

His jaw clenched as she pushed him. Goaded him. *But was it too far?*

She hoped so.

Silence was all she heard and a laugh came bubbling up despite her best attempts to choke it down. She felt the shift in him as a wrath like he'd not unleashed before started to fall upon him, but she wasn't afraid. No, she was far from it.

Quinn leaned forward into his strength, reaching up to grab him by the jaw. She formed an 'O' with her lips and blew out a breath of black magic. Playing with him. Toying with him.

It fanned around his face, touching his skin. He inhaled sharply and a glint of the monster in him looked out.

"Why do you do this?" he asked her through gritted teeth, struggling with control. "Why do you push me to my breaking point?"

The answer was easy.

"Because I want to see what happens when you finally snap."

It seemed those words were the shears she'd been looking for all along.

His lips came crashing down on her own. She bit into the plump flesh, drawing blood. Copper tasted in her mouth as she pulled on his bottom lip, sucking at it. He groaned, the hold on her throat turning possessive as she fisted both her hands in his hair and pulled sharply.

"*Saevyana*," he murmured, pulling away from her kiss. She felt his stubble along her jaw and then at the hollow of her ear. "Do you know what that means?" he asked her, his tongue skimming the edge of her lobe. He pulled it between his teeth and sucked once. The sensation made her lips part as heat stirred within her. The place between her thighs grew damp.

When she didn't answer, he gave a sharp bite and the breath hissed between her teeth.

"Tell me. Do you?" he commanded.

"No," she answered, breathing heavily.

He chuckled and the sound unsettled her as much as it excited her. "*Saevyana* means *my cruel woman* in Trienian," he whispered. A shiver ran through her as the hairs of her arms lifted. "That's what you are, Quinn. *Mine*. My vassal. My right-hand. My fear twister." He pulled back then and looked into her eyes. She saw flames and shadows there. She wondered if he was at the edge of dancing with Mazzulah. "You push, and you push, and you push, until you give me no choice." His fingers went to the ties of his cloak. Within seconds it dropped away, pooling at his feet. "Remember that."

Lazarus grabbed her hips and lifted her. Her back slid up the wall as his body caged her in, his form moving between her legs. She wrapped them around his waist, the heels of her boots digging in as she pulled him tighter just as he pulled her. She reached up, fisting his dark hair in one hand. She leaned in and licked the place where his shoulder met his throat.

Lazarus stiffened.

One of his hands moved to grip her rear, the other coming up to pull at the edge of her tunic covering her shoulder. She savored the sharpness of the cold on her skin as he pulled the cloth to the side. His stubble brushed over her bare shoulder.

"You let a man bite you here once," he said. His teeth came down hard, sinking into her flesh as he gripped her hips, moving them against his own. Quinn gasped. "I don't want to see anymore marks on your skin unless I put them there."

She felt hot and cold all at once, unsure how to process the meaning behind his words.

He meant to claim her. To possess her. And in this way, she would let him.

But she had to draw the line somewhere.

"You can't control that," she whispered as he licked over the bite mark. It hurt, but it was the good kind of hurt.

Quinn moaned against him, and instead of biting him back, she sucked on his skin, eliciting a groan in return. "Quinn . . ." He said her name in anguish, his shaft stiffening. He pressed into her and she urged him on, writhing against his hardened length, chasing that building pressure inside her.

"Mmm," she hummed back, working her hips against him. "See how giving I can be when you don't make demands," she started. The wall disappeared from behind her, and with it, her leverage. His arms became steel, holding her mere inches away as he carried her toward her childhood bed and dropped her unceremoniously. "If you walk away right now—" she started to snap.

He stood over her, massive in size, imposing in demeanor, and dangerously destructive in his gaze. The things he promised to do to her with his eyes alone made her settle back on her forearms and spread her legs in invitation.

His expression hardened into something almost angry, but he remained where he stood, reaching for the hem of his tunic. He pulled at the fabric, revealing a lot of scarred and yet flawless skin. The lines of his hard muscles drew her attention as much as the faded white marks and puckered edges where blades had touched him. Lazarus pulled the belt from his trousers and her heart leapt up as he came to kneel on the ground before her.

"I'm not walking away, and neither are you," he said.

Blood pounded in her ears as he reached for the hem of her tunic and lifted it over her head, tossing the clothing aside. He leaned forward—his palms settling on her knees and sliding up her legs. They ran over her hips, one resting on her flat abdomen, pushing her back—the other coming to settle over the damp spot of her trousers. He pressed down, sliding his hand back and forth and she arched her back, breathing hard. He unlaced the ties and then gripped the edge. Lazarus pulled them down, only pausing to remove each of her boots, until they were free. She lay clad in nothing but her undergarments as he leaned in. She felt the stubble of his beard against the inside of her thigh and she jumped. Lazarus must have known it was coming because he placed both hands on her hips, holding her still.

He moved to the apex of her thighs as Quinn propped herself up on her forearms, looking down to see his eyes closed as he ran his nose up and down her body, inhaling deeply.

"I'm going to take you with my fingers and then I'm going to taste you," he told her. She didn't reply, all the sharp quips she loved fleeing her as he tugged the fabric aside and ran two fingers through her folds. "And when you're ready, I'm going to fuck you like I've been wanting to for months."

She couldn't hold in the gasp as he shoved two fingers inside her and rapidly pulled them out. Her chest rose and fell with heavy pants. Lazarus repeated the motion. He grinned at her callously as he did so, stirring the heat inside her but never extinguishing it. He put his fingers in her and drew them out, building a steady rhythm. She started to rock her hips, wanting more from him.

"I'm ready," she moaned. "Let's get on to the part where you taste me—"

His reply was immediate, and his fingers pulled away.

"No one marks your skin but me," he said, completely serious. "Tell me that."

"No," she bit out, trying to pull away.

He chose that moment to place his thumb over the little bundle of nerves, swollen and greedy for his touch, and it only took two circles of his thumb for her to start quivering.

"Lazarus," she groaned.

"No, *saevyana*." He stopped and the fire flamed. "I want something from you, not just your body. Promise me no one else will mark you."

"Why are you talking so much? I want you to fuck me." She squirmed, using her feet to clasp his sides. Lazarus chuckled.

"I plan to," he said, leaning forward. He blew on her little nub, pushing two fingers inside her as he did. "Once you tell me that no person will mark your skin but me."

Quinn growled, thrashing her head. "No one marks me unless *I* want it."

"Then why is my bite on your shoulder now?" he asked.

"Because I let you," she snapped back. She sent a thread of fear at him and Lazarus growled.

"And will you let anyone else?" he asked, refusing to be swayed. She let another flick of fear shoot from her fingertips and he bit her swollen flesh. Quinn's legs shook as she shot upright completely, her hands coming down to grab his hair.

"Maybe. Maybe not," she said, pulling his hair hard but pushing him closer with all her strength. He sucked once and her hips bounced. Then he pulled away despite her hold, the wetness from her opening glistening on his lips. "I want you. You want me. Stop pushing for something I'm not willing to give. My body is my own, and for this night I'm letting you do what you want with it—but I'm not giving anything more."

He looked at her, his jaw clenched. "What if I offered something in return?"

She eyed him warily. "Like what?" she asked, more out of curiosity of how much this was worth.

"I won't let another mark me either," he said. "Only you, if you give me the same."

She stared at him for several seconds. "One night is all I'm up for. If you want to let some other woman mark your body, go for it, but I won't be manipulated into giving you more power than you already have." Lazarus frowned, his grip on her hips tightening.

"I could make you give it to me," he said.

"You could try," she nodded. "But you know that I won't give it."

He let out a frustrated growl and she nudged her body closer, moving to wrap her legs around his massive form. Still gripping him by his hair, she used her strength to pull their bodies flush and rub up and down him. "I could make you beg," he said, his own resolve weakening under her touch.

"Give me pleasure. Give me pain. I like both. But I will *never* beg."

He wrapped his arms around her, gripping her backside with one large palm. He dragged her up and down the front of his body and she moaned. His other hand skimmed up the side of her body, grasping the side of her undergarments and ripping them clean from her skin. She planted the balls of her feet in his lower back, working her warm heat over the front of his pants.

Lazarus groaned, nipping at her neck. It was sharp enough she knew he cut skin.

He was serious about intending to mark her.

She was equally so about allowing him this night, but nothing more.

It seemed he accepted that when he reached between their bodies to unlace his trousers. He pulled back, putting enough space between them that she could see his face as he pulled his length free.

The eyes that met her own were savage, primal, and entirely focused on her. He leaned forward, pushing their chests together as he guided her back toward the bed. She wasn't even fully against it when she felt the head of his member at her opening and then Lazarus thrust, entering her with a single movement.

Her lips parted at the sheer size. *Gods above . . .*

He pulled out and thrust again, his own hips hitting hers with such power the entire bed frame shifted and hit the wall. Quinn moaned, widening her legs to accept him and Lazarus took every inch, hard and heavy as the fire in her veins burned hotter and hotter. She clenched his hair to try to pull him down to her, but he didn't budge, instead punishing her at an angle that dragged him over her sensitive flesh.

Quinn began to pant, and he watched her, lips parted as she felt herself approaching the brink.

"I'm close," she moaned.

"I know," he answered back, gruff but not near so far gone as she. Lazarus moved one hand from her hip and ran his finger between her folds. He circled the source of her pleasure once and she shattered. Her legs shook as her back arched. Wetness flooded between her thighs and through it all her body sucked his shaft hard. Lazarus groaned, slowing his movements as she clutched at him as tightly as her shaking limbs would allow.

When the shudders faded, he pulled back, still hard and ready. She lay there, watching curiously as he stood and removed his trousers the rest of the way before coming over to her. She tilted her head, and he answered the unasked question.

"I get one night," he said. "I'm having you in every way while I can."

He flipped her over and then grasped her waist, pulling her up and back. She lay on her knees with her backside in the air and her face pressed down into her childhood bed. She only had to adjust herself, moving up onto her elbows.

Lazarus entered her from behind.

And Quinn let him. He took and took and took, marking her flesh and stealing her pleasure. Lazarus fucked her like he was chasing his demons.

Maybe they both were.

Moonlight filtered in through the window. Lazarus' hand around her waist was tight and possessive. She slipped from his arms and shoved a pillow into the space her body had occupied—trying hard not to look at his face as she did so.

Lazarus hadn't been gentle. Not when he took her from behind and came inside her while whispering her name like a prayer to some dark god. Not when he grew hard again and took her on her back once more, breaking the bed. She felt herself growing damp again as she silently sat at her desk, recalling how he'd bent her over it, and when her muscles couldn't hold up against his brutal thrusts —he'd resulted to fucking her against the wall.

Lazarus took her on every surface of her childhood room, including the floor before they'd finally collapsed in her tiny broken bed. She waited hours, and in that time he'd only woken once to fuck her again before falling into a deeper sleep.

The place between her thighs was sore. Quinn had little doubts that the journey coming would be difficult in those early days, not just for Risk, but her as well. He'd fully and thoroughly marked her body, and that wasn't counting the biting bruises that now lined her thighs, her backside, her breasts, and her neck.

Quinn shook her head, opening the desk drawer. She pulled a piece of stationary from where she'd left it as a child, plucking a well of ink and quill along with it. She stared at the paper, not sure of the words to say that would cool his rage when he learned what she'd done. After tonight, Quinn knew she couldn't just leave without word—or he would hunt her. Possibly to the edge of the world.

She couldn't have that. Not right now.

So, Quinn told him the only thing she could that might appease his anger.

The ink was still wet on the page when she stepped into the night.

By dawn the next morning, Quinn Darkova would be long gone.

An Oath of Return

"*Release your creatures into the night. When they return, your bond will be stronger for it.*"

— Lazarus Fierté, soul eater, heir to Norcasta, impatient warlord, soon-to-be king

"THE SUPPLIES ARE LOADED," DRAEVEN'S WORDS infiltrated his head as Lazarus stood at the edge of the dock with his back to the large vessel. "Lazarus?"

"I heard you," he said.

"What are you looking at?" Draeven turned toward Liph and examined the scene before them, but it was evident he couldn't see whatever Lazarus was seeing. Perhaps it was because Lazarus was not truly seeing the city at all. In fact, while his focus rested on the N'skaran capital, in his mind's eye, he saw something more. A lavender-haired beauty as wicked as women came—vicious and brutal in her violence as he was.

"Lazarus?" Draeven continued to pester him.

With gritted teeth, he turned away from the city and looked at his left-hand. "What?" he barked.

"Where's Quinn?" the man suddenly asked. "We're about to finish loading and head off."

Lazarus stiffened. "She's not coming." He turned and headed for the edge of the plank leading onto the deck of the ship.

"What?" Draeven snapped, hurrying after him. "What do you mean she's not coming?"

"She will catch up with us in Norcasta," Lazarus replied as his boots hit the deck.

"Is that smart?" Draeven asked hesitantly, looking back over him as the N'skari dock workers began to take the plank, letting the flat wood fall from the edge of the ship's side as the ship crew set to work on preparing for their departure.

"Whether it is or not, it is how it will be. She is

not returning with us on this journey. Drop the subject."

"She left, didn't she?"

Lazarus cursed him silently. He sometimes forgot how perceptive the younger man could be despite his sunny disposition. Casting his old friend a dark look, Lazarus stepped up to the edge of the ship and returned his attention to the coastline. "She will be back," he said. Though, truth be told, he wasn't completely sure who he was trying to convince—Draeven or himself.

Draeven hummed as he turned, leaning his waist back against the edge. The vessel jerked and pulled away from the docks, the eyes of the N'skari down below watching them distrustfully. Lazarus wasn't surprised that none of the councillors had shown up to see him off. *Well, almost none . . .* he amended as Verniez Laltihr lifted his hand in farewell. The lone councillor had promised, in as much broken Norcastan as he'd been able to muster, that he would study Lazarus' language so that—upon his next return—they could have a true conversation without the need for a translator. If anything, the man's willingness to acknowledge him as authority made Lazarus more suspicious. And yet, there was also a trust there. He knew the man would hold to his word. As would the rest of the Council. They had no choice, after all. Quinn had ensured that.

Lifting his attention from the man below to the horizon, Lazarus let the sun wash over his face, warming it. Empires rose and fell upon the Syrian Continent and, thanks to Quinn, his was on the rise.

First the Ciseans. Then the Ilvan pirates. Now N'skara. The first alliance to hold all three in nearly a millennium.

"What do you think, Lazarus?" Draeven asked.

"What?" Lazarus looked back, noting the man's expectant gaze that meant he had missed a good portion of whatever Draeven had said.

He sighed. "I asked what you thought about Claudius."

"Claudius . . ." Lazarus repeated. The man behind the rise of this alliance. The spark that had flamed his position of power. The King of Norcasta.

"Last we heard, his illness had taken a turn for the worst," Draeven reminded him.

"Yes." Lazarus nodded. "I received a raven shortly before we left Ilvas. I suspect that my ascension to power will happen not long after our return."

Draeven snorted. "Who knows," he replied, turning to cross his arms and lean heavily over the side as his eyes found the bits of ice in the water below—less and less as they were further from N'skara. "Perhaps you'll be king before you even reach the homeland."

"Perhaps," Lazarus agreed quietly.

"If you're worried about her, don't be," his left-hand said. "Quinn can handle herself. It is us who will have more pressing problems if Claudius does indeed die before we return."

"The blood heirs will not be able to hold the crown once the lords are made aware of the alliance I now hold," Lazarus said dismissively.

"I wasn't talking about the lords," Draeven replied. "I hear rumors from the south, and after what happened in Ilvas . . ." He trailed off.

"He won't make a move yet," Lazarus said.

"He's angry at you," Draeven said. "And has an empire of his own now to back his words if he chooses to do more than a few half-effort attempts at murdering."

"He wasn't trying to murder me," Lazarus said

instantly. "He was trying to get my attention, which he has."

"How do you know?" Draeven asked.

"Nero was like a brother to me once. I know him as well as I know myself. He's testing me right now. Seeing how close I'm paying attention," Lazarus said. "Believe me when I say this, Draeven, he's not our biggest concern just yet because he hasn't begun playing the game. We'll know when he has."

"How?"

Flashes of city painted red ran through his mind, but he pushed them back and said through clenched teeth, "We'll know."

Draeven sighed. " I hope you're right, for all our sakes."

Draeven left him at the helm with a heavy exhale, keeping his arguments to himself as he strode away. Lazarus looked out over the water as thoughts of Nero and returning to Leone fell aside.

He was ready to get back to his kingdom. That was prevalent in his mind, but not so prevalent as the paper in his pocket. Reaching down and letting his fingers skim the edges, he sucked in a breath as if he could feel her power even through her last note.

. . .

By the time you read this, I will be gone. When I see you next, you will likely be king. For now, though, Risk needs me. She needs a cure to her pain and that is something she cannot find if I am with you. This is not a goodbye. I will be back. Until next time, my King.

- *Quinn*

A SIMPLE PROMISE. AN OATH HE WOULD NOT ALLOW her to break.

He believed in her written vow. Even had she wanted to, Quinn could not stay away for long. Her blood contract to him prevented it. She would not escape him, his *saevyana*. She may be running now under the guise of helping her sister, but she would eventually return to him. He knew she felt the call in her veins just as he did.

She was his, and soon enough, she would come to realize just what that meant.

A New Beginning

"Life is a circle. While all things must eventually come to an end, so too must they begin."
— *Quinn Darkova, right-hand of Lord Fierté, fear twister, white raksasa*

Quinn looked out over the ravine, past the sleeping city of Liph, to the docks at the edge of her vision. She could barely make out the black sails, but they were there.

The ship she was supposed to be on.

"To think that I've spent my entire life here and never really lived," Risk said, sitting in front of her on the saddle. Her younger sister sat astride the great mount she'd taken in the dead of night. They set out long before dawn and were already well up the mountain when the time came that they were supposed to be at the docks too.

"You have," Quinn nodded. "But it's not the past that matters now; it's the future. You have to choose to live—to really live beyond what the world has taught you." She kept her eyes on the horizon even as she spoke.

"And if the world hates me for who I am?" Risk asked, tapping her horns. "For these?"

"Then let them," Quinn answered. "Better to fear you than to destroy you."

Risk snorted. "You say that because you're a fear twister."

"I say that because I've been enslaved, imprisoned, accused of trying to kill a queen, fought men and monsters alike—and throughout it all people have hated me." She paused, feeling Risk's eyes on her. "I'm alive today because I turn their fear into strength. You will learn to do the same."

"And if I don't?" Risk asked. "If I fail?"

"You won't," Quinn said, certain of that. "If your goal is to live above all else—you'll find a way. The only question is, are you ready to truly start living *for yourself?*"

"I am." Her sister's gray hands wrapped around the reins, knuckles white. Risk meant what she said, though, and Quinn knew deep down that while the journey ahead was a long way to go—she would make it. They both would.

"Then let them hate you. Let them love you. Let what they think matter not. If they try to end you, we'll crush them all. It's as simple as that." Risk shivered, but reached to hold Quinn's hand tightly.

They watched together as Leviticus' eye peaked over the horizon. The sky bled red and violet before tapering out into a deep blue. It was the light of a new day.

A new time.

And for some—a new life.

Quinn waited with bated breath for what the ship would do. As the sun inched up into the sky, it didn't take long. The sails unfurled, and while she couldn't see the people from her spot on the mountain, she wondered if a certain nobleman was watching on the deck—seeking her as she watched him set sail.

Quinn turned over her free hand, the one where his signature was scrawled. The letters glowed for a brief second and she smiled, knowing that when she returned to him he'd be a king.

And she'd be his right-hand.

"Where do you want to go?" Quinn asked as she took the reins and turned them away from the sun and sea. They had a long ride ahead of them through the mountains.

"Anywhere," Risk answered. "Anywhere but here."

In the distance, a bird cawed. She didn't have to look, for a silver feather drifted on the wind and up the trail. Perhaps a god had led her home, but without doubt, she knew that one was also leading her south.

To where her and the man she served would meet again.

To be continued . . .

Quinn and Lazarus story continues in :
For King and Corruption
Dark Maji Book Four

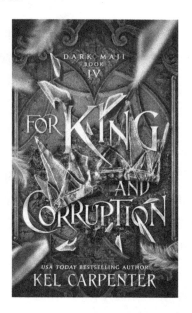

Also by Kel Carpenter

Ongoing Series:

—Adult Urban Fantasy—

Demons of New Chicago:

Touched by Fire (Book One)

Haunted by Shadows (Book Two)

Blood be Damned (Book Three)

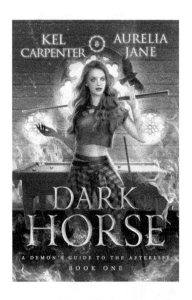

—Adult Reverse Harem Paranormal Romance—

A Demon's Guide to the Afterlife:

Dark Horse (Book One)

Completed Series:

—Young Adult +/New Adult Urban Fantasy—

The Daizlei Academy Series:

Completed Series Boxset

—Adult Reverse Harem Urban Fantasy—

Queen of the Damned Series:

Complete Series Boxset

—New Adult Urban Fantasy—

The Grimm Brotherhood Series:

Complete Series Boxset

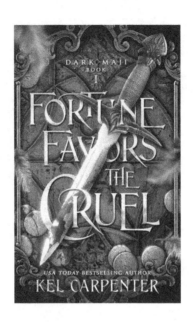

—Adult Dark Fantasy—

The Dark Maji Series:

Fortune Favors the Cruel (Book One)

Blessed be the Wicked (Book Two)

Twisted is the Crown (Book Three)

For King and Corruption (Book Four)

Long Live the Soulless (Book Five)

About Kel Carpenter

Kel Carpenter is a master of werdz. When she's not reading or writing, she's traveling the world, lovingly pestering her editor, and spending time with her husband and fur-babies. She is always on the search for good tacos and the best pizza. She resides in Bethesda, MD and desperately tries to avoid the traffic.

Join Kel's Readers Group!

Acknowledgments

This was the "for love" book of the Dark Maji series. It's the concept that started it all. A woman who was forged from a dark past, and instead of being broken, came back to break those who dared try.

Thank you to my editor for all of your hard work. You go above and beyond.

Thank you to my friends and family for your unending support.

And thank you, dear reader, for following Quinn and Lazarus to whatever dark places their characters take me.

CPSIA information can be obtained
at www.ICGtesting.com
Printed in the USA
BVHW091106260122
627129BV00008B/186